MR. WRITE

A SUNDAES FOR BREAKFAST ROMANCE
BOOK ONE

CHELSEA HALE

crescendo
INK

To David—my very own Mr. Right—who has made my dreams come true since we first met. Life with you is my favorite Happily Ever After. Loves!

FREE BOOK

Join Chelsea's VIP Reader's Club and receive a free book (http://smarturl.it/claimyourfreebook).

CHAPTER ONE

Liz Montgomery bolted into the football stadium as the third quarter began. She stopped to catch her breath, the air around her felt thin. She was late. Parking six blocks away and running the whole way in sandals had left her winded. Her dry throat ached for relief. She'd need more than a week back from her summer in Texas to acclimate to the altitude in Boulder.

The familiar smells of concession food, warm air, and hot metal mixed together, inviting her to the nearest line to quench her thirst. It was a perfect day for the first game of the season. Her twin brother, Grip, played quarterback for the University of Colorado, and she watched every game. Normally.

This was all her brother, Sam's fault. Why had he called an hour before the game to tell her he was bringing someone for her to meet? Maybe having her roommate hide her car keys was a bad idea after all. She had only wanted to be twenty minutes late, not miss the first half of the game.

The single concession stand employee juggled filling drinks and taking payments. She craned her neck toward the field, squinting against the late afternoon sun. The cheering grew louder, and she scowled at her obstructed view of the field. If she hurried, she might catch the instant replay on the screen.

Every guy Sam had set her up with, since breaking off her engagement two years ago, was disastrous. She thought after the last time, Sam had taken the hint that she could find her own dates. Apparently not.

She tapped on the counter after getting her large root beer. "Could I get a lid?" Liz asked, as she paid the cashier.

"Sorry, all out. The other concession stand might have one." The cashier returned Liz's card.

She sipped her drink down a few inches. The bubbly liquid soothed her dry throat. She descended the stairs toward her front row seat. CU's fight song broke out, and the entire home section stood and cheered. Everyone stopped to join in, and Liz watched the instant replay of a sweet tackle on the big screen.

Ahead of her a guy went down the stairs, his sculpted shoulders boasted regular use. Even from her raised angle, he seemed tall. She didn't pay attention and lost her footing. She collided with the muscles in front of her. His nachos flew from his paper tray. Root beer shot out of her cup, showering them both with the brown sticky carbonation. The guy grabbed the handrail and steadied them both. His strong hand wrapped around her arm, keeping her upright.

"Are you okay?" he asked.

Liz stared into the most beautiful green eyes she'd ever seen. Her mouth hung halfway open as she studied the man who broke her fall. He was probably around her age, mid-20s. His strong jaw was evident as the corners of his mouth lifted into a smile, pushing his left cheek into a deep dimple.

She blinked, raising her gaze to his eyes again. They held amusement. "I'm okay," she said. "I'm so sorry. I'm not sure what happened."

"You knocked me off my feet," he said.

Heat crept up her neck. "Under different circumstances those words would thrill me." She laughed until she looked down at her shirt and his, then groaned. Normally fans wore black. Of course, she and the guy she drenched were the only white fish amidst the sea of black and gold logos. Stickiness settled on her skin.

If Sam wasn't already suspicious that her late arrival meant she was avoiding the set up, he might wrongly assume she purposefully spilled on herself to make a bad first impression. There was only one thing to do. She'd head back up the stairs and buy a new shirt.

"Thanks for breaking my fall." Her voice came out breathy. The air really was thinner.

"Anytime."

She arched an eyebrow. "Anytime? Really?! I don't think I'll plan that move again."

3

It was his turn to laugh. A deep, rich laugh that made her want to join in.

Instead, she crossed to the other side of the stairs. "Thanks again."

"Wait. Where're you going?" he asked. He picked up his ruined paper tray of nachos and followed her back up the stairs.

Her pulse quickened. He was good-looking and had a beautiful voice. But she was about to be set up with someone. Not that she was looking forward to that. On second thought, maybe this was an okay situation after all. A little flirting with a stranger may be the exact thing to turn Sam's friend off. She'd find her own dates.

She paused on the stairs, then turned to face him. "I'm going to buy a shirt. I just got here and should look presentable coming to the game. It's kind of important."

"So important that you came halfway through?" His eyes sparkled.

She smiled. "Can you keep a secret?" She ran up the stairs, hoping he would follow. Once at the top, she headed toward the nearest apparel store.

"You tell secrets to people you don't know?" He stood next to her.

Liz held out her hand, her mouth going dry. "I'm Liz. Nice to meet you."

He shook her hand firmly. "Tyler."

"Now that we know each other, I can tell you my brother is setting me up today. I'm not really in the mood for that, so I didn't want to be on time." She grabbed two fitted CU shirts from the rack. "Which do you like better? The light or the dark?"

"The dark."

"Me too." She put the light one back, and grabbed a matching men's in large, and headed to the register.

"So, you decided to blow him off?" His eyes widened.

The cashier rung Liz up. "Of course not. I can't show up late to the game for no reason." They walked out of the store, and she handed Tyler the men's shirt.

He thanked her for it, then nodded. "What's your excuse?"

She pulled the tags off her shirt. "My roommate hid my car keys really well this time, and it took me longer to find them than I anticipated."

"Why would she hide your keys?"

Liz grinned. "I asked her to. If I can't find them, it's a perfectly legitimate reason to be late to a game. Only it took longer than I planned to locate them."

Tyler raised his eyebrows.

She held up the merchandise bag. "That's why I had to come buy a shirt. If I show up drenched, my brother is bound to know I'm trying to make a bad impression when I meet his friend. He'll assume I've spent the first half of the game avoiding him."

"Which you did."

She rolled her eyes. "Yes, but *he* doesn't need to know that."

"And you're telling me because?"

She shrugged. "I spilled my root beer on both of us and needed a new shirt."

He stopped in front of the concession stand. "I'm going to get some food. Mine was soaked by a beautiful redhead," he said. He ordered nachos and a large root beer.

She pushed her card toward the cashier before Tyler retrieved his. "Let me. I owe you."

"Thanks." He held out the tray covered with chips, cheese and jalapenos toward her. "Want some? You bought them."

She gingerly lifted a nacho with three jalapenos on it, and popped it in her mouth. She swallowed it without batting an eye at the heat. "You don't prefer your nachos drenched in root beer? It's all the rage in some parts of the country." Her lips twitched. She couldn't help teasing him. He intrigued her.

"Which parts exactly?"

"Oh, you know, everywhere but here. But we're catching on to the trend." She gestured between them. "Someday we might be thanked for capturing the vision of the drink spilling movement."

He leaned toward her and whispered conspiratorially, "Until the drink spilling movement becomes a trend, you can have this all to yourself. Deal?" He handed her the root beer, brushing her fingers with his. "It was nice meeting you, Liz. I better get back to the game."

She raised her eyebrows at him and nodded. He probably had a girlfriend. It didn't matter. After this encounter, she would tell Sam that she was perfectly capable of finding her own dates, if she wanted. "And I better go change. Thanks for the root beer."

"Thank you for the amusement."

Liz changed her shirt, and surveyed the status of her hair—root beer had matted down the top in a sticky mess. She blotted her curls with wet paper towels but not much could be done to salvage them. The hand dryer would only make it frizzy. She pulled her thick, red hair into an unflattering ponytail.

She was on auto-pilot as she made her way to her season-ticketed seat. Her thoughts wandered repeatedly to Tyler, and to how she would let Sam and his friend down easy.

"Where have you been?" Sam didn't remove his eyes from the game. "Grip is tearing it up out there. The game is practically over and you never miss a game."

Liz sat down in her seat. She was surprised that Sam, and not her blind date, sat in the chair directly next to hers. On Sam's other side, her blind date sat between her parents. He was turned away from Liz, talking to her mom, on the far side of the group. The thought that her blind date chatted it up between her dad and mom made her blood pressure rise. Why wasn't he sitting next to Sam?

She couldn't imagine the stories her mom might have shared while she hadn't been here. Had she known she wouldn't have been late. She was overanalyzing—Sam wasn't the best judge of her taste in guys. Besides, she'd worked up the exact thing to say, and thanks to Tyler, she didn't even have to make the story up.

"Sorry I'm late. I couldn't find my keys. And I had to park six blocks away. Then I ran into a guy and we hit it off. It wasn't too long, but we shared some food and talked. I know you want to introduce me to your friend but I met someone. I'm sorry to trouble you."

Sam burst out laughing. "He must be amazing if you don't want an introduction." His voice was louder than it needed to be.

Liz touched his arm, lowering her voice. "Sam, I'm thankful you look out for me. It's sweet of you. But I really can find my own dates."

Sam surveyed her pulled back damp ringlets. "So, this guy you ran into, you're going to date him?"

She shrugged, watching a lineman intercept the ball before she answered. "Maybe."

He smirked. "Did you give him your number?"

"No." The flaw in her logic came forward.

"So, the next time you run into him, you'll give him your number, then?"

She dropped her voice to a whisper. "Yes, I will. But fine. I'll meet your friend."

Sam laughed. Hard.

"What's so funny?"

"I wasn't trying to set you up."

"You weren't?"

"Do you remember the last time I did that?" He shook his head. "I won't go there again."

Confusion wrinkled her brow. "But you told me to look nice. And said you had someone you wanted me to meet. At the game."

Sam wiped a pretend tear from his eye. He waved his fingers over her. "You coming straight from a shower with wet hair and a CU shirt is you looking nice? You wanted to make *this* your first impression?"

She held up the CU store bag. "No. I had a root beer mishap. So, I did damage control." She pushed against his arm.

Sam raised his eyebrows. "You spilled root beer on the guy you hit it off with?"

Liz couldn't read his expression. But she decided it was best to answer the questions about the root beer before it became a family dinner conversation topic she'd never live down. "Drenched us both. But since I assumed you wanted to set me up, I didn't want to show up soaked."

Grip scored a touchdown, and Liz jumped to her feet with the rest of her family as the crowd went wild.

Sam cleared his throat. "Let me introduce you to the person who caused you to change." Sam motioned to his dad, and his dad swapped seats with the stranger.

The guy in the dark shirt turned toward her. Liz saw his face for the first time and her eyes widened. What were the odds? Tyler stared back at her.

"Tyler." Sam gestured toward Tyler. "This is my sister, Liz. She had some trouble getting here. Apparently, she was *also* drenched in root beer. Liz, this is Tyler, Kyle's biographer. He's in town to interview us."

Kyle's biographer? Sam really *wasn't* trying to set her up.

Her older brother, Kyle, was two years older than Sam, and starting his sixth season of stardom in the NFL. Being MVP, running a successful charity, and following in his older brother, Ron's and dad's footsteps made him someone people watched. It wasn't surprising that he'd have a biography done.

Sam nudged Liz with his elbow. "I let him borrow my hat since I didn't want him to look *unpresentable* when you finally showed up."

Liz glared at her brother, then looked back at Tyler.

Neither of them moved, then Tyler cleared his throat, and extended his hand, for the second introduction of the day. "Tyler Lakewood. A pleasure to meet you."

Her burning cheeks flamed with blotchy heat. "And you," she mumbled.

Sam exchanged seats with Tyler. "Don't get any ideas about dating my sister, Tyler." Sam leaned toward them, out of the hearing range of Liz's parents. "Apparently, she ran into someone on her way in, though she didn't give him her number. But next time she sees him, she's going to fix that, since they hit it off. I don't set her up anymore." He turned and started talking with their dad.

Could her older brother be more annoying?

Liz kept her gaze on the field, keenly aware of Tyler's gaze in her direction.

Tyler's arm brushed against hers on the armrest between them. "Sorry," he whispered.

"For what?" Sure, her brother could embarrass her, but mostly she embarrassed herself. What were the odds that Sam wanted to introduce her to the same person she ran into?

"I had no way to explain the root beer on my shirt. I told Sam. I didn't know you were related to him."

But Sam knew. He'd been laughing at her the whole time. That's why he wanted to get the story out of her first. She'd give him a piece of her mind later.

Liz shrugged it off. Then she whispered, "Please don't tell him that I had my roommate hide my keys. I might not be able to live that part down."

"And the part about your number?"

She laughed. "I'll live that part down. Besides I don't need his advice on who I should date."

"Of course, you don't."

"Kyle didn't mention he was having a biography done." She knew he'd had several offers by biographers to get his story over the years. But he hadn't once mentioned that he was going to have a biography written this season.

"It was only finalized a few days ago."

She surveyed Tyler again. He couldn't be much older than she was. Why in the world would Kyle choose him to do the story? She was less than a year from graduating with her Masters in English. She wasn't really expecting to write Kyle's book herself, but Tyler couldn't have more experience than she did, could he?

Time to put her journalism skills to work. "How many biographies have you published?"

He cleared his throat. "It's actually a new genre for me. I'm ahead of schedule for production, and my agent thought I could get the majority of this written without any impact to my other projects."

A new genre? Meaning his experience wasn't high. She hoped he wasn't a groupie, of Kyle, or her family, but she had to know. "Why did Kyle choose you?"

"You object to his choice?"

Object to Tyler? No. But she'd seen how her family's fame affected others. "Just curious. If you've never written a football player's biography before, why are you interested now?"

Tyler shrugged, turning back to the game and cheering for Grip, though Liz missed the play Tyler cheered for. "Kyle asked me. It's different enough from what I regularly write, so I thought I'd give it a try."

"Give it a try?" Maybe he was just another fan of her brothers, looking for an in. That was too bad. She couldn't be interested in someone who only wanted to be connected to her family. Not again.

"Let's save the book inquisition for later, and you can give me your phone number now, like you told Sam you would the next time you saw me." His green eyes sparkled.

Heat flared on her cheeks.

His smile revealed his dimple. "I can always get it from Sam."

If he wasn't interested in a connection to her family, she'd give him her number in a heartbeat. But as Kyle's biographer? "I can always ignore you if you do."

"Did you have a sundaes for breakfast kind of day, or are you going to tell me all of the details now?" Jenny sat on the couch and looked up from her book when Liz entered. She owned a four-bedroom house, and she and

12

Liz had been roommates since freshman year in college. Eating sundaes for breakfast and swapping date stories was Liz's favorite roommate tradition. "New shirt? Or did you change again before you left?"

Liz dropped the bag containing her stained shirt, then joined Jenny on the couch. "It's new. Are Mandy and Coco still out?" She wanted to tell all of her roommates at once.

"You *do* have a story. I knew it." Jenny jumped up from the couch and headed for the kitchen. Her straight chestnut hair swayed perfectly in its place. No crazy hair for Jenny. But then, Liz's hair standing out like a bonfire in a sea of blonds and brunettes was the reason Jenny remembered her years ago.

Jenny returned with two pints of ice cream. "Coco has a wedding shoot tomorrow that she's preparing for. Mandy still has jet lag."

"You'd think with the amount Mandy travels that she'd be used to jet lag by now." Mandy was a travel companion and tour guide for elderly women who wanted to see the world.

Jenny handed Liz her favorite. Ben and Jerry's Salted Caramel Core. "Spill it. What happened? Did Sam pick out a great blind date? You were gone a while."

Liz scooped some of the center caramel out of the carton, and swirled it around the white ice cream. "Funny thing actually. Sam wasn't trying to set me up. I spilled my root beer on a hot guy as I headed to my seat. I confessed that you hid my keys, bought myself a shirt and his replacement food, including a root beer for me, come to think of it. Then I went and changed. We hit it off for the few minutes we talked to each other."

"Liz is back in the dating world? I'm shocked."

"Hardly. I'm open to dating. He did have gorgeous green eyes though."

"Did you give him your number?" Jenny sat with her spoon halfway between her carton and her mouth.

"Before or after he ended up being the guy Sam wanted to introduce me to?"

Jenny squealed. "No way! You told him you were avoiding Sam's friend, and he ends up *being* Sam's friend?!"

"Thankfully Tyler isn't really a friend. He's Kyle's biographer, in town to interview all Kyle's family and friends for the story."

"Ah. This is perfect."

"Come again?"

"You're hesitant to date guys your brothers set you up with," Jenny said.

"Wouldn't you be?" Sam meant well, but he'd introduced her to Rick, and after she broke off the engagement, Sam seemed to make up for that introduction with several others who weren't her type either.

"It's not your fault Rick," she said, pausing to make several gagging sounds, "was a jerk, and I can see why you're hesitant to date your brothers' friends." Jenny ate a few more bites of ice cream.

"It's nice that someone understands," Liz said. Rick had cared more about becoming a member of her family than he had about marrying her. He'd wanted an automatic 'in' to the stardom fame that was the Montgomery legacy. Consequently, she didn't want to date guys who were already good friends with her brothers.

"Yes, but here's the thing. Tyler *isn't* a friend of Sam's, so he can hardly be put in the same category. Besides you said he was good-looking, and he sounds nice. Plus he had a sense of humor about the whole root beer spill."

"He *was* nice. That only makes the whole thing worse." The idea of dating Tyler before she knew how he was connected to her family warred with the desire to stay strong on her policy.

"What's his name? I'm going to google him." Jenny pulled out her phone.

"Tyler Lakewood. This is his first biography though, so I'm not sure what genre he's in."

Jenny scrunched up her nose. "Yeah. I'll say he doesn't write biographies." She scrolled through the screen and mumbled, "Pen name Ty Lake—that's clever. Best-selling author. Check. Epic fantasy is mostly what he does. He's published a lot for only a decade in the writing business, but he doesn't look old. Twenty-six. He published his first book when he was in high school. Wow. You should pick his brain about his writing career. He'd be fascinating to talk to."

"I'm not going to date someone who is working for my brother. Or someone who is connected to my family."

Jenny picked up the cartons of ice cream, sweeping them back into the kitchen. "It's still a funny story. It goes on the list." She stood in front of the fridge and wrote on the whiteboard.

Liz rolled her eyes. Jenny loved lists and loved to overanalyze. Without the regular schedule of all the roommates swapping stories, creating a list was the easiest way to catch everyone up.

Intrigued by what Jenny read about Tyler, Liz pulled up Tyler's author page on her phone. She browsed through his different series and clicked on the first one in his newest trilogy. She'd started writing a fantasy novel back in high school, after she stopped cheerleading. Maybe that was why she was interested in Tyler's book. Before she could think too much, she bought the digital book.

Jenny came back from the kitchen. "So, when's your interview?"

CHAPTER TWO

Tyler parked his car in the circular drive and headed up the massively wide steps leading to the double front door. The Montgomery house was by far the largest on the block, spanning several acres. Mature trees bordered the property, and a tall stone fence surrounded the area. Every home in the gated community had manicured lawns.

The early September sun hovered in the air, warming his back as he grabbed the knocker on the dark wood door. His sister's spacious house, nestled in Boulder, was tiny in comparison.

He knocked and waited, but there was no answer. He checked the address again. This was the Montgomery residence.

"Let me guess. You used the knocker." A familiar feminine voice came from behind him.

He turned around to see Liz smiling at him, her eyebrows raised, as she slid her white sunglasses from her nose to perch on her head. She wore dark gray capris that hugged her, accentuating her curves, and a sophisticated yellow blouse.

Sam had described his younger sister, Liz, like she was still in junior high—with wild, tangled hair, and more than a little awkward. But her curls were tamed and with the sun on her back, her hair seemed to glow. He was drawn to red hair. From the bio sheets, she was twenty-three and studying English. Just three years younger than Tyler. And Sam hadn't mentioned anything about her fun personality or her beautiful smile.

She tilted her head at him, and he realized he never answered her question.

"I'm not supposed to knock?"

Liz's wedge sandals added an extra two inches to her 5'7" height. She looked at him with golden hazel eyes. Had he seen their color yesterday?

"Knock all day if you want. But if you want to come inside, ring the bell. I always walk right in."

"No one comes if you knock?"

"Knocking is great, in theory. But really, not in a big house, with a busload of boys. Things are always knocked about. So, it's silly to run to the door every time there is a knock or a sound." She opened the door, and pushed it forward. "Come on."

Tyler stepped through the front door onto marble floors, with intricate molding everywhere. Vaulted ceilings graced the entryway. Large windows let in natural light, showcasing the grand piano off to the right. A large vase, filled with fresh cut flowers, was nestled in an alcove next to the spiral staircase. It wound up to a bridge over-looking the entryway and the opposite side of the house, presumably another living room. A water feature, lit by spotlights, hung on the wall, letting water run down the slate rock. It produced a calming environment.

"You *live* here?" It was the only thing he could get out of his mouth. In New York, he lived in the fast lane of the rich and famous, the rub your shoulders against everyone else's rich shoulders, kind of living. But being raised by his sister and brother-in-law, life never looked like this in Colorado.

Liz laughed. "No. I grew up here." She squinted around the entryway. "I guess it's a little over the top."

Liz's mom, Helen, came bustling around the corner, wearing an apron and a warm smile. Her auburn hair was pulled back in a bun, giving her a little more height on her shorter frame. Tyler guessed she was 5'4".

"Oh, Liz you're here. I was getting worried you might not make it. Appetizers come out in a few minutes." She turned to him. "Tyler, it's nice to see you again, dear. We're glad you can join us for dinner. You'll have to fill us in on your plans for the interviews. We're all dying to know how we can help you." With that she turned and left, probably toward the kitchen.

"That's mom. She loves being interviewed. Loves talking about herself and her kids. Talks too much, if you ask me." Liz followed her mom.

Tyler smiled. "She'll be the first I interview then."

"Don't believe everything she says. Get her journals and binders. Those have the accurate information."

"Binders?"

"Every bit of information you want, it's in there. She goes through each article written about her sons, and does a detailed analysis on its accuracy. It also included her descriptions of her video catalog she kept for the boys when they were younger. But when she's in storytelling mode, she doesn't consult her binders." Liz's eyes twinkled. Helen sounded very invested in her sons' careers.

They gathered in the formal dining room. The table held twenty, and more than half of the places were set. Place cards stood beside each dessert fork. He found his name, and sat next to Liz.

Tyler was grateful for the bio sheets Kyle sent him of his family, though everyone introduced themselves as they sat down. Tyler mentally went through what he knew about them as he chatted with everyone at the table.

His dad, Jack, at the head of the table, was a seasoned football star and coach. In his early years, he was a legend in the NFL. The media had buzzed about his decision to retire early to coach high school. He coached all of his boys in the sport he loved. It was admirable.

His oldest, Ron, played in the NFL before a torn ACL brought him into early retirement. Ron's wife sat next to him, with their three boys and a girl scattered between their uncles and aunt.

Kyle, the second oldest, was starting his sixth NFL season next Sunday, and lived in Texas with his wife.

Sam had opted to go into sports medicine to stay connected with football. Grip, or Luke, was Liz's twin brother. He was playing his final season at CU. Recruiters were his focus this year. Liz was finishing up her Masters at CU.

Dinner was loud. Tyler glanced around the table as he ate his food. Everything was formal, but still felt like home. He fingered the place card with his name elegantly scripted on it. *Everyone has a place.* It was a nice thought, a great thought to apply as a biographer, but not in his personal life. It was times like these that he wondered what his life would have been like if things were different.

His memories as a six-year-old of what his life was like before his parents died were dim. Being raised by his sister wasn't a bad thing. He was grateful to her, and to his brother-in-law Jim, but with his sister standing in his mom's place, he felt like an only child, even after his sister had her own daughter. He pushed the memories aside, as he ate another bite of steak.

"This is delicious," Tyler said to Helen. "Gourmet cooking."

Helen beamed. "I'm glad you like it. Steak and grilled potatoes with asparagus is one of my favorite menus. Of course, I suppose in New York you get this kind of thing all the time."

He'd had his fair share of good New York steaks, but this was better. Maybe it had something to do with the surrounding company. "Not even close. It's the best I've ever had."

"Don't overdo it, or you'll never be allowed to leave," Liz whispered from behind her napkin.

"But it really is delicious."

"I know." She smiled at him.

"So, Liz, did you give that guy you met at the game yesterday your number?" Sam said from across the table.

Tyler glanced over at Liz. Yesterday she seemed interested in him, until they sat next to each other during the game. She intrigued him and his pulse quickened while he waited for her answer.

Helen chimed in from the end of the table. "Liz! You didn't tell us you met someone at the game yesterday! How did it go? Do you think you'll date him? When can we meet him?" Helen leaned over and whispered loudly to Tyler. "I care about all my children, but there's something about wanting your only daughter married."

Tyler glanced from Helen to his other side where Liz sat. Her cheeks pinked, but otherwise seemed steady. She narrowed her eyes at Sam, and he looked away.

"Meeting guys, instead of watching your brother play?" Grip seemed good natured as he laughed from the other side of Liz.

"The only person I remember meeting yesterday was Kyle's biographer. But I'd be happy to introduce you to Tyler, if you need another introduction." She gave a tight-lipped smile and continued eating.

The conversation moved to Tyler and to his plans for the biography. Questions flew at him for the next few minutes, and he finally put down his fork, realizing it was impossible to eat while answering everything.

"My goal is to interview each family member in-depth. I have some questions, but I don't want you prepared ahead of time. I want to get a fresh perspective on Kyle as a person, and as a brother, and as a son." He had everyone's attention. "I'd also like to spend time shadowing Jack and Grip, and get some insights on what Kyle's time in both high school and college were like."

Grip nodded. "Sounds like a good idea."

After dinner, everyone went outside. The backyard was immense. Trees and gardens bordered against the stone wall, leaving over an acre of running space in the middle of the yard. The covered deck had several different levels to it, and at the bottom sat an outdoor oven and fireplace.

"Up for some football?" Grip asked Tyler as they walked down the deck steps.

"With your family? I think I'd better be the spectator."

"Frisbee football then. I'll go easy on you. C'mon."

The game started up. Grip and Tyler were on opposite teams. Liz came out, setting drinks out under the covered patio. After half an hour, he found her again, at the table playing dominoes with her niece.

Tyler gulped in air and grabbed a drink from the table. "Is your family competitive at everything, or just things with football in the title?"

Liz smiled. "You don't think my brothers got lucky at a sport they're obsessed with, without a healthy dose of competition, do you? You're the biographer, so you'll come up with your own conclusion."

"You didn't sign up for an interview slot, speaking of," Tyler said, noting the list on the table.

"None of your times work for me. How about you ask me your questions right now?" She picked up another domino, setting it next to a small pile, and directed her attention to the little blond girl. "Good job, Linny. Great stack."

"I can work around your schedule. I'm here for a month." He watched Liz play with Linny. Both of them had curly hair. The smell of coconut entered his senses as he leaned toward her.

Liz pointed at the paper in his hand. "You're trying to pack them all into one week?"

Tyler shrugged. "Next week I'm shadowing your brother. I want to leave time to do follow-up interviews, if needed. My Tuesday is open during the day."

She shook her head. "I have class, then work. That pretty much sums up all of my days."

"Lunch then?"

"I could do lunch Wednesday," she said, laying a piece down on Linny's pile. The girl jumped off her lap, spilling the dominoes everywhere, and ran down the steps.

"Lunch Wednesday," he repeated, wishing tomorrow was Wednesday. "I'll need your number now."

Tyler was up before the sun Monday morning, and drove into Denver. This was the last week of summer break before high school started, and Jack Montgomery agreed to have Tyler shadow him for the football team's early morning practice. He met Jack half an hour early to get a tour of the weight room, and see the school.

"You've got a nice setup here," Tyler said, admiring the room. Everything was in pristine order, and professional. Not your typical high school feel. "No wonder you turn out more college and pro players from this high school than others."

Jack beamed with pride. "It's been a home away from home for the last nineteen years."

"Mind if I take a few pictures?" Tyler asked, studying the wall with all the previous years' team photos. He stopped at the photo where Kyle was named the MVP.

"Not a problem," Jack said.

They walked outside. The sun wasn't visible yet, but the sky had lightened. They headed toward the field, where a few high schoolers stretched.

Jack put a hand on Tyler's arm to stop him before they entered through the gate. "Now. I'm giving you fair warning. I'm the coach. This is my team. You're welcome to observe and take notes. I'm not going soft on these boys because you're here.

"They've got a game to get ready for, and life to prepare for. Today will be typical of any other day I've had here since I started coaching. If you have questions, I'm happy to answer them after practice, but I'll be ignoring you until then."

Tyler nodded his agreement. "I really appreciate you letting me come. Thank you."

Jack shook Tyler's hand. "Sitting on the bleachers will be a good spot for you."

Tyler spent the next three hours analyzing the practice. Jack was a legacy in his own rite. Though he was intense with the boys, he was a good coach. Someone they obviously looked up to. Tyler scribbled notes about the impact such a father and coach would have on Kyle's life. This was part of the untold story. Lots of people knew that his dad had coached Kyle, but watching Jack coach brought a whole new meaning to Kyle's story on the impact Jack had.

Sadness welled inside of Tyler as he scanned through his notes. Biography writing on a close-knit family was going to be rough on his psyche. He imagined all the time Jack spent with his boys, teaching them how to throw a football, or watching a game together. He could see Jack staying late after practice to spend extra one-on-one time with each of his sons, until after dark.

He was given a rare opportunity to dabble in a different genre with a high-profile star, who wanted an artistic edge in his biography, not a stuffy version of himself. The timing of Kyle's book lined up perfectly in between his own projects.

Tyler had already planned a month vacation time with his own family in Colorado, and with Kyle's family so close to his own, it was going to work. This was no time to feel sorry for himself. He had a great life. He pushed his feelings aside.

CHAPTER THREE

L iz headed to work after her only class on Wednesday morning. The first day back since she returned from Texas seemed heightened with anticipation. Maybe it was her lunch interview with Tyler. She straightened up her desk, and unlocked a small cabinet that held her personal pictures and supplies while she'd been gone. The morning sun filtered through the conference room creating a cheery atmosphere in the law office.

"Liz, you're back!" Marcus Williams, the second Williams in Williams, Williams, Foster & Stone stood tall in the doorway to his office, a smile on his tanned face.

"So are you, Mr. Williams." Marcus had been traveling since Liz arrived back in town.

Marcus arched an eyebrow. "So formal after a summer away? Marcus suits me better. There is already a 'Mr. Williams' around here." He nodded his head toward the end of the hall, where his father, Brent Williams resided for most of his waking hours every week.

"Okay. Marcus."

"I'm glad you're here today. My first day back from vacation is always a dreaded day for me." His dramatic eye rolling coaxed a smile from her. Same Marcus. "Let's get the brain dumping session over with so I can go back to pining for a few more days on the beach."

Being Marcus' personal assistant was rewarding and paid well. Twenty-five hours a week wasn't full-time, but she stayed caught up on her work. Marcus planned around her football commitment and she was rarely expected to work weekends.

He worked long evenings occasionally, but five hours a day was easy to fit in with school, and when days were lighter on work or when the semesters were more intense, he had always cut her some slack and she studied while he was in meetings.

Liz grabbed a legal pad and ballpoint pen and followed him into his office.

Marcus rolled up the cuffs of his tailored button-down dress shirt, and loosened his tie. *He's relaxed from his vacation. Good sign.* She geared up for a long session of note-taking. Mounds of paperwork littered his desk, but he leaned back in his leather chair and rested his elbows on the armrests, putting his folded hands beneath his chin—his thinking pose.

"How have you been, Liz?" His tone was light.

"Um, I've been good. How about you?"

"Good? You sum up a whole summer away with

'good?' I'm a lawyer, Liz. I like verbose lexicon. Humor me."

"It was exciting to get away. I helped Kyle with Happy Moments. It's a big job getting ready for his annual Thanksgiving Charity Ball. The charity sponsored building an elementary school in Ecuador, and I went down for two weeks. It was intense work. No time to go to the beach."

Marcus nodded. "I should be back on a beach right now. Thanks for the reminder. I'm glad you had a good time, and that you're back to work. I've missed you."

"I am an excellent filer, if I do say so myself," she teased.

"Yes, and the temp agency couldn't keep up."

"From what I hear, you've gone through a lot of assistants while I was away." Turnover could be high in a college town, but Marcus wasn't hard to work with.

"Four in three months. Save me from training more."

She tapped her pen on the blank canary paper in her lap. "I won't last another second around here, unless you put me to work."

Marcus leaned forward in his chair and rested his folded hands on the desk. "Let's get started. But I want to hear details about your work with Happy Moments another time."

Two hours later, Liz came out with stacks of paperwork and seven pages of action items on her to-do list. She couldn't believe the amount of work ahead of her. Marcus had paralegals in the office, and mostly her job consisted of keeping his brain from exploding with tasks and ideas. It kept the job interesting.

"Did he hold all that work for you for the last three months?" Bertha's eyes widened as she saw the stacks Liz carried out from Marcus' office.

Bertha had worked at WWF&S for over a decade as Mr. Stone's assistant. Bertha's southern drawl drew Liz in, making her wish her whole life was set in the South. The phrases "honey lamb" and "sugar pie" warmed Liz's heart and made her think of Bertha as the office aunt, the kind who would have worn a sun hat accented in silk flowers, and would've pinched Liz's cheeks with her freshly lacquered red fingernails if Liz was in grade school. She smiled wide to hide the giggle that threatened to emerge at the thought.

"Bertha, I've missed you. How did I go so long without seeing you?" She couldn't keep in a grin now, as the sun hat image appeared in her mind.

"Oh, sugar plum, you are a ray of sunshine and apple blossoms, and I want some serious details on all your goings on with Happy Moments." Bertha swiveled her chair and went back to her typing after Liz nodded an agreement.

She dropped the last stack of papers on her desk, took a sip of water and lost herself in the familiar work.

An hour later she filed the unorganized paperwork Marcus handed her. The temp employees really made a mess of the personal paperwork Marcus kept. Had Liz known it was going to be chaos in her filing cabinets, she would have come in the last two weeks to make sense of it.

"Bertha, have you seen the Wentworth paperwork anywhere?" she asked, as she came back from the hallway with the overflow of files.

Bertha was talking to Tyler. He looked good in jeans and a polo.

"Hi, Tyler." She smoothed her hands down her skirt. Bertha was bound to be disappointed when Liz explained there would be no interesting details from a working lunch.

"I'm underdressed in this office," he said. "Ready for lunch?"

"Yes." She grabbed her purse, ignored the looks from Bertha, and locked her computer. "Let's go."

Tyler opened the office doors, car door, and restaurant doors for her. She was impressed he was a gentleman.

"I know you're short on time for lunch, so this was a close option," he said, opening up his menu, once they were seated.

"I love this bistro. Great food and atmosphere," she said.

They ordered, and Liz said, "So tell me about you, before you interview me. You're really Ty Lake?"

"You googled me, did you? That's my pen name." He smiled.

Her cheeks heated. Technically Jenny had looked him up first. "I couldn't find you under Tyler Lakewood. I wanted to see what you wrote."

"Mostly I write epic fantasies."

"That explains why Kyle picked you then. Next to football, and of course Kandice, he loves reading and that's his favorite genre." She pulled out her phone, and hovered a finger over the screen. "And it says here that you published your first book before you learned to drive?"

The waiter came with a plate filled with three types of hummus, pita bread, and sliced vegetables. "On the house, for Ty Lake. Manager's order."

"That's very kind. Thank you," Tyler said to the waiter. He pushed the appetizer toward Liz. "Google me later. It's embarrassing to watch others read about you on the screen when you're sitting right here."

She could relate to that sentiment. Of others having the advantage over her of her name and interests because she was the kid sister of famous football players. She dropped the phone into her purse. "Fair enough. So how did you meet Kyle?"

"He contacted me a few years ago, and asked if I was interested in it. At the time, I was in the middle of a series, and our schedules didn't align. But we've stayed in contact.

"About a month ago, he called me again to see if I was still interested. I'm ahead of schedule for my next trilogy, and had planned on coming to Colorado to spend time with my family, and take a small vacation. When he told me that his family was also in Colorado and it would work for me to interview them, I jumped at the chance to extend my trip."

She nodded, and ate an appetizer. Kyle assumed that everyone would be available for interviews without even asking. Annoyance filled her. It would have been nice to have a heads up that Kyle was going to be involved with a biography on top of the Happy Moments responsibilities. She spent the entire summer planning for the Thanksgiving charity dinner and ball, and she still had several things to coordinate.

It was time to tell Kyle that she needed to be done with Happy Moments. She'd make it through Thanksgiving with a brave face on, but it was a demanding job, and with finishing grad school and her law office job, she wanted to focus on her writing. With all of the work she put into her online articles for Happy Moments, she was sure she could secure one of the internships to write for the *True Story* magazine.

The food came. "This looks so good," she said.

"Mine too." He pulled out a black leather-bound notebook. He opened to a blank page and put Liz's name on the top. "I have lots of questions."

"Fire away."

"What did you do with Kyle growing up?"

"He'd take me and Grip to bookstores. Almost anytime we passed one, we'd stop. It was a tradition. He would give us a clue to finding an interesting book or some random topic. First person to find a book that fit the description won."

"Kyle said you're the reason he and Kandice got together. Tell me about that."

Liz smiled. "That's a long story. You could probably write a whole book on that subject."

"Kyle said you were instrumental."

"Oh, I was. Most people need a good push in the right direction." She leaned forward. "My superpower is matchmaking."

"Tell me more."

Liz knew there wasn't enough to do the story justice. "I'll tell you the whole story, but we'll be here through dinner if I start on that subject, and I have to work this afternoon. Any other topics?"

He studied his notebook one more time. "How does Happy Moments work exactly? Are you the main player for that? Kyle told me you're the resident expert on it."

"That's about right. I manage a portion of it. It's great experience, I suppose. It does a lot of good. Kyle had a dream when he was younger about giving back. His wife Kandice was the one who brought the dream to life though, and then Kyle ran with it. He couldn't decide what he wanted to focus on, so he named it Happy Moments, because that was the common denominator on everything he wanted to do and give. And it's incredible."

He took a few notes, circling a few words, and under-lining others, as she gave more details about the different projects Happy Moments had sponsored. He tilted his head, watching her as she took another bite of her sandwich.

"What about switching genres? How has that worked?" she asked.

"Genres switching will keep things fresh. Hopefully. I have a grasp on storytelling when I'm writing up all of the characters and their backstories. It's been interesting to think about tying in a compelling story when it has to be true, like in a biography. I think I'm up to the challenge."

"Your epic fantasy style is so tight."

He raised his eyebrows at her.

"I may have finished two of your books since Sunday night," she confessed. "You write so seamlessly. You've definitely got the art down."

"Thank you."

Liz felt her ears warm. She hadn't meant to gush about him. "When did you know you wanted to be a writer? I mean, was there an actual specific moment that you can point to? Did you always know you wanted to live in New York?"

Tyler shifted in his seat and cleared his throat.

"Sorry. I didn't mean to put you on the spot. You probably get pestered with questions all the time. I'm an English major, but you already knew that. Anyway, it's a business I'm interested in."

He smiled sadly. "You're fine. My parents died when I was six—"

"I'm so sorry," Liz said.

Tyler nodded. "My oldest sister Stephanie graduated

from high school the same year I was born. She and her husband Jim took me in, after my parents died. They have Cassie, who has been more like a sister to me than a niece. I was so young that processing the traumatic experience at such a young age was impossible.

"I was in a deep, dark place for two years until I attended an author assembly at school. He talked so passionately about writing to express feelings. I came out of the gym with a desire to write and use my imagination to create my dreams, and hush my nightmares. It gave me something to focus on when I couldn't cope with the floods inside of me. In sixth grade, my favorite teacher praised my writing and read an entire short story of mine to the class."

Words alluded Liz. She hadn't expected such a personal story from him. She put a hand over his, wishing she could transfer comfort in the touch. "That's a great story."

"It's defined my career. Something good is created from bad experiences. I weave that theme through my epic fantasies. Life can still be rewarding, even when it's painful."

Liz felt the connection between them. Since Saturday they had hit things off, even with her brother teasing her. But this felt more like a date conversation than a working lunch interview. The idea both scared and excited her.

"What's your dream with writing?" Tyler asked.

Not even her family really understood what she

wanted to do with her major. But she thought Tyler would. "I want to write for the *True Story* magazine."

"Really? In New York?"

"Yes."

"That's great. I didn't peg you for a big city sort of girl."

She shrugged. The big city wasn't the problem. It was supporting her family while living far away that she wondered about. "Who knows. Maybe I'm not."

"But *True Story*. That's big. Tell me about it."

She leaned forward, excitement prickling her skin. "I've already gotten a few letters of recommendation from my professors. They're glowing evaluations about my writing and work ethic. Most of the application is finished."

"Are you nervous about their on-demand story?"

Liz was impressed that he knew about their application process. Within a week of the application being received she would be given a story assignment and a firm deadline of twenty-four hours to get it done. "It's a little daunting."

"Their signature style of weeding people out is effective. They want to know how you'll perform if you write for them. It's one thing to have a perfectly polished piece you can perfect over a few weeks or a month. They like to see excellence under a deadline, without any way to prepare for the topic."

She leaned forward. "I can handle the pressure."

He smiled at her. "You'll do fine, then. Let me know

if you'd like me to look over your article. Happy to help. It can be a tough business."

The idea of asking him about her work sent a nervous skitter around her stomach. He was a best-selling author, making a name for himself early in his career. The significance of his offer wasn't lost on her. "Thanks. I'll keep that in mind."

Tyler paid for the meal, and they headed out to his car. "I still have a few questions to ask you about Kyle."

"You know you're going to need more than a week to get all of these stories." *And maybe we'll do lunch again.* The idea had her head buzzing.

He helped her into the car. "You're probably right. And Sunday is a big day at Kyle's house?"

Liz wasn't sure if she was more excited to go to Dallas for the game, or that Tyler was coming too. "Yes. You'll have the inside scoop on what life is really like. The first game of the season is a big deal. We don't take the jet for all our trips, but it's used for the first game. It's nice when it's a home game. Kandice throws a huge party at their house afterwards."

"I'm looking forward to it."

Me too. Liz's phone rang. "Well speaking of, it's Kyle. Do you mind if I take it? He never calls me during the day unless it's urgent Happy Moments business."

"Sure."

"I was just talking about you," she said into the phone.

"All good things, I hope." Kyle's voice came across the line.

"It'd serve you right if they weren't, springing a biographer on all of us without time to prepare," she teased.

There was a pause. Not good. "Sorry about that," he said. "But it may not matter at the moment anyway. I might have to pull the idea."

"What's wrong?"

"It's our permit for building a school in Peru next summer. Legal is trying to get the paperwork done, but the country's regulations for outside help has been delayed. They're estimating not getting the all clear until after Christmas."

"I filed those at the beginning of the summer. How did they get dropped like that?"

"I'm not blaming you, Liz. This isn't your fault. Peru's process is going through restructuring. All paperwork is shut down. Not just ours. If we proceed right now, legal thinks we will be rejected automatically. We don't have a choice. We have to start over."

"Wait. Start over start over, or start over with a different country? Can we go back to Ecuador and build another school there?" She could hear the panic rising in her own voice.

The school had been her idea. Her decision to push this for next summer. It sounded promising. She wanted to do something big. Something that would make Kyle proud of her. But, as the project came crumbling down she felt surrounded by the dust of failure. Nothing achieved.

"We need to start over."

She couldn't tell Kyle she wanted to quit Happy

Moments while he was stressed about his next year's plan. They planned their schedules almost two years out. There were no warning signs that this project would fall through.

"Can we pull out another project idea? Announce something over Thanksgiving, or maybe hint at the project and announce officially when we get the approval?"

"I know this is disappointing for you. I wish we could make it work. But we can't announce next year's plans based on speculation. We always announce at the Thanksgiving Charity Ball. It's one of the main purposes of the night. We need to come up with a new plan."

"A new plan? In less than three months? The coordination of our previous plan took the entire summer, as my full-time job, without school and work. Can't you pull in anyone else to do this?" She didn't have enough free time to be able to tackle this alone. No way. She'd have to tell Kyle she was out, even if it disappointed him.

"I already tried. Our three other assistants can't work during the fall semester. I know this is a huge burden on you. Will you think about it? Even just going through our old brainstorming notes? This weekend is the first game of the season. As much as I want to only focus on the charity, I have a season and a game starting. I won't be able to think about this for at least another four weeks, and by then it's too late."

Liz put a hand to her forehead, knowing she might have to drop her classes to be able to fit the work in that he was asking of her. It was a huge sacrifice. Next summer's internship at *True Story* would be off the table if she didn't graduate in May. It'd be another year of pushing things off. "Okay. Let me think about it, and we can talk again after your game this week."

"You're the only person I can count on for this. I owe you one."

"You owe me more than that. Good luck on your game. I'm cheering for you." She would make this work. Somehow.

She hung up after saying goodbye, only then realizing that they were parked in front of her law office.

Tyler raised his eyebrows. "What's wrong?"

She explained Kyle's end of the conversation, and how her plans were a complete bust. Without time to start a new proposal and get permits and regulations, their big event would have to be domestic. It wasn't the worst thing. There were plenty of opportunities to serve and help, but she had less than three months to plan and execute the majority of it, so they could announce at the charity dinner.

Recounting the story to Tyler gave her a clear picture on how much work had to be done.

"On the plus side, there's still two weeks to drop classes and get a full refund." She gave him a wry smile.

He held his hand out to stop her on the sidewalk. "You wouldn't really cancel your classes for this, would you?"

It wasn't her first option, but her brother was counting on her, she'd do what she had to. She'd help build Happy Moments up and didn't want to see it come crashing down because she was too selfish to sacrifice for it. Happy Moments helped so many people, and Kyle needed her. She shrugged. "Something you'll probably pick up on while writing Kyle's biography is that family comes first. Even at the expense of others. It's part of being in the Montgomery family."

He held open the law office door for her. "Can I pick your brain again about Kyle this weekend?"

She felt warm inside remembering their easy conversation. Talking to him again sounded enjoyable. "I can always gush about how awesome my family is."

Tyler's smile didn't quite reach his eyes. "I'm looking forward to it. Thanks."

She sat down at her desk, and despite Kyle's news, she was unable to wipe the silly grin plastered on her face away. Tyler was a gentleman, attentive, and had offered to help her with her writing.

"Someone looks like they had a good lunch," Bertha said, clicking away at her computer.

"I really did." The idea surprised her. When was the last time she'd had such an enjoyable working lunch? Tyler had cared about her problem and her stress. Even though he didn't have to. Conflicting emotions ran through her. He was attractive, and there was no denying the connection between the two of them, but she still wanted to connect with someone who wasn't already connected with her family.

"I could eat that yumminess up all afternoon." Bertha wiggled her eyebrows, and laughed. Typical Bertha.

~

A whole summer of work lost. Liz parked the car, and headed toward the house. She opened the door with more force than necessary and pasted on a smile when she saw Jenny and Mandy in the living room chatting.

Jenny didn't miss a beat. "That bad, huh?"

"My permits for Happy Moments haven't been approved yet. Legal won't guarantee they will be secured by Thanksgiving. I have to start completely over."

"Bah. Too bad that's not my area of expertise," Jenny said. She had taken the bar this past summer.

"What are you going to do?" Mandy asked, looking up from the notebook she was drawing in. She was always doodling or drawing something. "Do you have a backup plan?"

"Not yet. Kyle wants me to rethink the whole thing."

"That's a lot of work," Jenny said, "You spent all summer on that. And last summer too. This is a huge time commitment."

"I know. But if I do something domestic, it should be quicker. And as long as I get the right ideas in place, most of the execution can be done after Thanksgiving."

"Let us know how we can help. I have a few weeks at home before my next work trip," Mandy said.

Jenny pursed her lips, then said, "Liz. This is a huge job to redo. How can Kyle expect you to do this alone?"

Liz blew out a breath. Kyle hadn't given her another option, so she'd have to muscle through. "I don't know."

43

For the next three days, Liz worked frantically, trying to come up with a solution for Happy Moments. She squeezed every inch of time in her schedule, didn't socialize with her roommates, did the bare minimum for her classes, and left early on Friday from work. Her *True Story* internship application collected dust while she thought about Happy Moments, but still couldn't come up with anything.

The fast-paced schedule of her life began to unravel. Every project couldn't be embraced whole-heartedly. Something had to give. She needed to choose. By herself there was no way she could graduate with her Masters and run Happy Moments. Forget being social. It was her sanity she needed. She'd talk to Kyle on Sunday after his game.

She worked a few more hours on Saturday night, then opened up her phone and continued reading Ty's epic fantasy novel, releasing her stress as she let herself be swept away in the story.

CHAPTER FOUR

S unday morning came early.

"You're sure you want to tag along for today?" Tyler asked his niece Cassie as they arrived at the airport. "It's not too late to back out." Cassie was a junior at CU.

When Kyle heard that Tyler's sister, Stephanie and her husband, Jim, were out of town for the weekend, he extended an invitation for Cassie to join Tyler at the football game.

"I'm good to go. Besides with mom and dad out of town, it's nice to spend time with you. You've been busy lately."

"You're gone all week long in classes and studying," Tyler said.

"Yes, but I try and keep my weekends free when you're in town."

"Sorry. I'm trying to fit in all of these interviews."

Tyler parked his car at the airport, and they unloaded their small day bags.

"Don't be sorry. I get to tag along today and spend time with you. It'll be fun."

They went through security, and walked down one of the terminals. Tyler hoped he remembered the right area to go for the personal jets. He was sure they were in the location Jack and Helen told him to meet everyone. He'd flown on personal jets before, but something about Liz's family owning one made him feel inconsequential. He was way out of his league.

"You're sure this is where we're supposed to meet them?" Cassie asked.

The terminal was deserted. Not even an airport employee was around. "I think so."

They chatted for a few more minutes, then Tyler spotted Liz coming toward them.

"You're prompt. Everyone else should be here soon."

Tyler made the introduction. "Cassie is my niece. She's only five years younger than me and goes to CU. She's more like a sister, really."

"Yes. You mentioned her at lunch." She cleared her throat. "It's nice to meet you, Cassie," Liz said. "I always picture nieces being younger. Mine is only two. I'm glad you could join us."

"Nice to meet you too," Cassie said.

The rest of Liz's family trickled in, and Grip came right over. "Liz, I didn't know you were bringing a friend."

"This is actually Tyler's niece, Cassie. She goes to CU. Cassie, this is my twin brother, Grip. Between you and me, he's probably the cooler half."

Cassie giggled.

Grip and Cassie started talking, and Liz moved over to Tyler and whispered, "And that's how it's done."

Tyler tilted his head. What did she mean? He doubted Cassie would say more than a few sentences to Grip. And the conversation would probably end at their majors and favorite place on campus.

Liz smiled, and kept her voice low. "Grip will be monopolizing Cassie for the entire day. I'll bet you anything."

Liz didn't know how introverted Cassie could be. "Cassie isn't a big talker. She's very shy. We haven't spent much time together since I've been back in Colorado. She'll probably spend all her time with me." He watched Cassie smile and blush as she talked to Grip.

Liz raised her eyebrows. "If you say so. But if she ends up in a conversation with Grip on the plane, I'm happy to answer more questions about Kyle. Unless. Did you bring a book or something?"

He was happy Cassie made a new friend so easily. He wanted her to have an enjoyable day. Maybe college life broke her out of her shell more than he realized. "I'm all yours."

The rest of the Montgomery family gathered, including little kids. They were in pajamas, holding onto blankets, and the little girl rested on her dad's shoulder.

Tyler smiled at the picture. The Montgomery family was big and welcoming. He was glad Cassie came with him today.

They boarded the personal jet. It was modern and roomy. Seating was on the perimeter of the plane, with an open layout in the middle. There were long couches and several swivel chairs.

"Have you figured out what your new project is going to be for Happy Moments?" Tyler asked Liz when they were settled in their seats.

"Not yet." She sighed.

During the flight, Liz was social with everyone, mingling with her family, and her parents and of course her nephews and niece. He watched all of the family interact from a distance. He took notes, focusing on the biography, but time and again his attention was drawn back to Liz, especially when she'd laugh. She had a beautiful laugh.

When they landed, they drove straight to the stadium. Since Jack was part of the Owner's Club, they had valet parking under the stadium, and a suite box reserved for them. The big screen TVs were mounted on all the walls, anywhere there wasn't a full floor to ceiling window, letting him see the game no matter what direction he turned. Tables were filled with catered platters of finger foods and desserts.

He pulled out a notebook to record his impressions.

Liz handed Linny over to Ron, then wandered over to him. "And this is why we leave early. It's a party before the game."

"It certainly is." With regular gatherings like this, no wonder they took the jet to be here for the first game of every season. More people continued to enter.

"Don't get the wrong idea though. We don't sit up here every time. Sometimes we sit in regular seats. It's our tradition to do that at least for the first half of the game on Thanksgiving."

"Only the first half?" An odd tradition.

"One year it was very cold in the seats, so we stuck it out until half-time, then came up here where it was warmer. We've done it ever since."

"I'll make a note," he said, smiling at her.

Kyle's older brother Ron came up to Tyler and they both filled a plate of food. "The food and the party are two things I missed out on while I was in the NFL. Kyle is in the locker room right now, mentally preparing for the next few hours, while we enjoy all of this." Ron gestured around the room, as more people entered the Owner's Club. It smelled of expensive food and leather. The plush chairs were set in groups around tables, perfect for conversation. Dozens of recliners faced the windows to watch the game.

Tyler took a seat next to Ron. "You miss playing though?"

"I took early retirement with my injuries. Of course, I

miss it. I sat out for a full season with a torn ACL. I was ready to be back in the game. And if that game wasn't football, I needed to get back in the game of life."

"But you made a full recovery," Tyler said. Was Ron concerned about reinjury?

"I did. And I could have come back. Maybe stronger." He looked toward the field. "Sometimes when I watch Kyle play, I wonder if I made the right decision. If I should have pushed through for a little longer." Ron's son sat in the chair next to Ron, and he ruffled his hair. "But then I remember my dad giving it all up because of his family, not because of an injury. He wanted to pass on his love of football to us. And he did that by being our coach, instead of being the star in the game."

Ron had a strong role model, and Tyler could see that Ron's mental toughness likely contributed to Kyle's success, too. "Sounds like you made the right decision."

He laughed. "And for the biography record, I'm okay that my younger brother has achieved more success than me. I knew it would happen when I stepped off the field."

"I'm sure your support adds to Kyle's success."

"He never needed my approval or support. He wanted to be his best and pushed himself without my encouragement."

Liz brought Linny over to Ron. "She wants daddy snuggle time."

"That's my cue." Ron stood and his son followed him. "Nice talking with you, Tyler. Let's turn my interview into a round of golf, I'd love to finish our conversation."

"Sounds good," Tyler said.

Liz sat in the chair Ron vacated, and whispered. "You must be a good conversationalist. Ron is selective on who he invites for a round at the Country Club."

"You can be the judge of the conversation. I have to interview everyone." Maybe Ron preferred a less formal interview style.

"He didn't have to invite you, and he did."

"Your family is very hospitable," he said.

She stood. "They are. The game is about to start. I always do a cheer with Grip. It's a twin thing. I'll see you later."

I hope so. He watched her with Grip. They did a series of fist bumps, and high fives. It looked like something they made up in elementary school, but it was endearing. He talked with several different people as he meandered through the crowds. Kyle's mom, Helen, introduced him to several different people, each time making a big deal about the introduction and how Tyler was a bestselling author. He should put her on his PR team, she was good.

The room exploded with excitement as the game started. Kyle's family gathered closer to the windows. Some other friends and colleagues of the family stood around the big screens. He settled into a leather chair that angled to the windows. Cheering erupted from everyone when Kyle scored a touchdown.

Tyler wondered if Cassie was having a good time. He had barely said a few words to her since they arrived at the stadium. He didn't realize how wrapped up he would get in his own conversations. She sat next to Grip on a couch. At least she wasn't by herself.

It was obvious Kyle's supportive family was a driving force in his success. He hadn't known that to this extent before he met them. Interviewing each of them would be more beneficial than he realized.

During half-time Tyler got more food. A few teenagers came up to him. One of them nudged the other and he spoke. "Are you Ty Lake?"

"I am." He smiled at them.

"I told you it was him," the other said.

"Could I get your autograph?"

"Of course." He tore a page from his notebook, signed it, and handed it toward them.

"You're my favorite author."

"Thank you." Meeting fans was an ego boost. He signed another piece of paper. "Here you go."

"You have a fan club," Liz said.

"Kind of a strange place for it," he said, though he'd been asked for autographs in stranger settings.

"Not a strange place at all. Lots of celebrities come here. It adds to the fun." She sat down next to him.

They talked and cheered together throughout the second half, and Tyler found himself wishing he'd sat next to Liz during the first half of the game too. She called several of the strategic plays, and yelled at the refs through the windows at the calls she didn't like.

Kyle played well. Tyler was glad they won their first game. It would set the mood for Kyle's biography.

~

The entire Montgomery family headed to Kyle's mansion after the game. The house bustled with people. Several others went outside and enjoyed the pool.

"Hiding for any particular reason?" Cassie came up to him. "Come join in. Grip is going to give us a tour before dinner." Cassie held Linny in her arms.

"I'm not hiding. I'm observing without getting in the way of the story," he said.

"I bet you can still enjoy yourself without changing the story," she said.

After a tour of the house, they changed into swimsuits and gathered outside with the rest of the party. The pool curved and a large rock cave at one end created a waterfall into the pool. A couple of boys played football on the grass, and some adults sat under umbrellas.

"Good game today," Tyler told Kyle. "You're impressive on the field."

"Thanks for coming, Tyler," Kyle said, shaking his hand. "It means a lot."

They grabbed some of the catered BBQ spread, and talked at a table under the covered patio. The more Tyler got to know Kyle, the more exciting this biography became for him. He watched how Kyle interacted with everyone. He was genuinely nice and friendly. He joked around, and drew others to him.

Tyler joined in swimming and different water games with the family. Kyle's wife, Kandice, also had a lot of her family over. Both families got along well and everyone seemed to have a good time.

Kyle and Tyler sat in the hot tub, and Liz joined them.

"How is the revamping of plans coming?" Kyle asked Liz.

Liz's eyes widened. "I've barely had a chance to think about it. I don't have much time to do this."

"Liz, this is priority one. I have to get this done. You need to help me. Getting Happy Moments back on track trumps all of your social activities."

Tyler thought back to his lunch conversation with Liz. It didn't sound like she had free time.

She squinted at her brother. "You think I'm blowing this off? I don't have a social life as it is. I've spent the last few summers donating all my time to this charity, and part-time before that. I'm working on it, but I still have a job, and classes. They take up all of my time. I told you I don't have time to do this by myself. I need help."

"I'm working on finding someone to help you, but I don't have extra time now that the season has started up. I'm under a lot of pressure, and I'm in the middle of coordinating for the biography."

Liz raised both eyebrows. "Which is your priority? The biography or Happy Moments?"

Kyle sighed and caught Tyler's eye. "Tyler, I want to get this biography out, but," he said, looking over at Liz, "She is right. I have too much going on. Until I get the Happy Moments figured out, I'm putting the biography on hold."

Tyler couldn't be hearing this. "So...you don't want me to write your biography?"

"I want you to write it, but I want Happy Moments fixed more. I'll compensate you for your work so far on the biography, and hopefully it won't be long before it works to finish it."

He wanted to do the biography, but this was his only window between his books that he could give this kind of attention to it in the next two years. "I'll help with Happy Moments," Tyler said.

Liz's jaw dropped. "What?"

"You want to help plan my charity service project?" Kyle's eyebrows scrunched together.

Ideas flowed into Tyler's head. He wouldn't mind spending more time with Liz. Though they barely touched on his interview questions, he wished he'd had more time during their lunch to talk. She intrigued him. "If I helped Liz get your project for next summer planned, could we keep the biography on schedule?"

Kyle nodded. "I'll compensate you for your time on Happy Moments, but that has to be the priority, before my book."

From the corner of his eye he saw Liz's face turn blotchy.

He didn't care about compensation. He wanted to get to know Liz better. "Whatever you think is fair."

"Will Happy Moments work with your deadlines?"

Tyler thought for a moment. His agent, Alex, would be furious if he was distracted with a non-writing project, but helping with Happy Moments was the fastest way for him to get back to writing the biography. "I can help. I had some ideas about helping children with literacy, or maybe improving communication skills through books."

Kyle tilted his head. "At this point, I'm open to anything. That's not our usual way of doing projects, but it could work. We need to have it in place before Thanksgiving."

"Kyle, I want it to go with our previous projects. Literacy is not something we can push from a small charity angle. There is not very good metrics to measure how we make a difference," Liz said to Kyle, though she kept her eyes on Tyler the entire time.

"Literacy might be a great idea. And we have a best-selling author who is willing to help. See what you guys can figure out."

Before they left, Tyler found Kyle in his massive library with dark wooden floor to ceiling bookshelves. Heavy curtains covered the large windows. It looked like he bought a bookstore and dropped it into his house. Tyler passed by a large globe on a pedestal, and several configurations of couches and chairs before reaching Kyle's desk at the far end of the room. Behind his desk several glass cases displayed footballs between the rows of books.

Tyler wanted to discuss biography angles with Kyle, but the timing was off. Happy Moments was the priority. "I'm happy to help with the charity, but Liz may not want my help."

"She'll get over it. Two years ago, she was engaged to the guy who helped her with a project. Since then she goes at life alone. But she needs the help. If Kandice wasn't expecting right now, I'd ask her to..." Kyle stopped, his eyes widening.

"Congratulations," Tyler said.

"Keep it under wraps. She wants to announce it big. First game of the season down. By next week, I might have a brain to think about it."

"She's not announcing tonight?"

"Not all of her family is here. We'll announce soon."

"I won't say anything about it." He wouldn't break Kyle's trust. "I think I can still work on your biography while helping Liz with Happy Moments."

"That'd be great. Liz wants me to choose between them, but I want both right now, and both are a big deal to me."

"I'll keep you posted on how it goes."

Kyle thumbed a book on the table next to him. "Can I ask you a favor? Will you let me know if Liz hits her breaking point? I'm not trying to stress her out, but there isn't anyone else I can rely on to do what she does."

"What about your other brothers or sister-in-law?"

Kyle shook his head. "The charity has been running under Liz's careful planning. She knows all of the ins and outs. Trying to train someone brand new in such a short time is tough. I hope you can stand drinking from a fire hose."

"It'll be fine." *Drinking from a fire hose?* What did he get himself into?

"I'm counting on you to let me know if Liz can't do this."

Tyler swallowed. It was sweet that he cared about Liz, even if Liz didn't see it that way. "I'll keep you posted."

CHAPTER FIVE

L iz, and her family left Dallas at 9:00 p.m. She slept on the jet, then drove from Denver to Boulder. She arrived home after midnight Sunday night. NFL games were a whirlwind, but life continued on in a different state on Monday morning. It was good to support her brother.

"Coco? What are you doing up?" Liz asked Coco, who sat at the dining table, her face illuminated by her bright laptop screen in the dark room.

"Couldn't sleep. Thought I'd work on a few more edits on my video. I've almost got it perfect."

Liz dropped her backpack to the floor and took a seat next to Coco at the table.

"Want to see a few clips?" Coco asked, playing with her short, dark hair between her fingers.

"Always," Liz said. Coco was a film student, and always worked on something creative. She ran a small business shooting wedding videos on the weekends. She made enough to put her through school.

"This was an impromptu assignment. We only had an hour from the time we were given the assignment until the time it was due."

"That's crazy."

"You're telling me. See if you can guess the theme." Coco's leg bounced up and down.

Liz liked Coco's enthusiasm about filming. "Okay." She watched a montage of a boy finishing a bowl of ice cream and a girl walking a dog. They didn't seem to go together. Coco's assignments were so abstract, while her own English major followed rules. She smiled at the irony. English rules hardly counted as rules, and more often than not there were several exceptions. Maybe abstract was the way to go. "Being happy?" she guessed.

"Not finished yet." Coco pointed to the screen.

A blackout faded into an old man buying ice cream, and an older woman snuggling a puppy. Another cut, and the young boy again, then the young girl. The montage continued. Liz wanted to wrap her brain around the deep thinking of this video. It was intriguing, but she stifled another yawn.

"It's reverse order. Or out of order. See, the old man is buying the ice cream, but it's the young boy who's finishing it," Coco said.

"Ah. I see. And the young girl walks a grown dog, while the old woman holds the puppy."

Coco nodded. "We all filmed the same four people. They went through the same motions with all of us filming, then we were able to have two minutes with each where we could have them do something specific, to get a few different angles—ones the other students didn't see. Now I'm putting it together."

"Would it make sense to put the old man first, then the young boy, so it's out of order that way, too?"

"I thought that might be confusing. But you like that idea?"

"You never know until you try it. It's a good start."

"I already turned in this version, but we have until Tuesday to make a second version. Then we'll watch both versions back to back and the class will judge on which one is more appealing—the one that we did in under an hour, or the one we took more time on."

Coco clicked off her screen onto another clip.

"It sounds cool, Coco. Sorry, I'm just tired." Liz yawned again.

"Speaking of, how was your day with the biographer?"

Her whole family was there. "It was a good day. I met his niece, who's twenty-one. Both of them were really sweet with my niece and nephews."

Coco nodded for more information.

"Kyle wants Tyler to help me with replanning the Happy Moments service project that fell through. At least brainstorming new ideas. I don't have time for all of it, so it'll be nice to get some help, I suppose."

"And you'll be spending more time with Tyler. That's exciting." She smiled and nudged Liz with her elbow.

Exciting. Nerve-wracking. And everything in between. She couldn't deny her attraction to him. Liz stifled another yawn. Her perfect excuse to get out of this conversation. "Maybe exciting. Maybe aggravating. He isn't catching the vision of it yet."

"I'm sure you'll help him with that."

Spending more time with Tyler had her insides jumping. "I'm going to bed. Good night." She barely made it to her room without tripping over her emotions tied up around Tyler.

On Monday evening, Liz came home late from work. She was in a great mood until she received a text from Kyle.

Checked status with Tyler today. He has some great ideas for Happy Moments. With his help, you should be able to get this done before Thanksgiving.

Great.

It was bad enough that she was attracted to someone who worked for her brother. Now she'd have to work *with* him. If Tyler cleared all of his ideas with Kyle *before* he talked to *her*—the person executing all the plans—he was going to drive her crazy.

Liz pulled out a head of lettuce from the fridge. "Salad for dinner tonight? I'm in the mood to chop something."

Jenny came into the kitchen and pulled out a few cucumbers and carrots. She put them on the counter, then took the lettuce away from Liz. "What's going on?"

Liz rolled her eyes. "Tyler offered to help me replan Happy Moments' service project for next summer. Kyle says he has some great ideas. Can you believe that?"

"That's great," Jenny said, missing Liz's sarcasm.

She grabbed the lettuce back from Jenny, and washed it. "Great? Great that Tyler is going to help? It's most definitely not great." She couldn't sort her feelings out, and Tyler made it hard to think. Concentrating on solving Happy Moments would be impossible.

"He's writing a biography for your brother. So, what? Heaven forbid you find a nice *helpful* guy, who has the ability to take some of the pressure off this huge project while you're in the middle of finishing up your Masters."

"Exactly." Liz shook the lettuce off, and chopped it hard against the cutting board. "I'm not looking for options here. I have plans. I don't want to run Kyle's charity full-time. After graduation, I'm heading to New York. I don't want to be tied to Colorado forever."

"All the more reason to let him help you."

"He probably wants to make sure that Kyle doesn't cancel the biography. It's not like he really wants to help me."

Liz's phone buzzed, and she read the text message and groaned.

"Who's it from? Grip or Kyle?" Jenny peeked over her shoulder.

She didn't recognize the number. "Probably Tyler."

Jenny grabbed Liz's cell phone reading the text aloud.

Can we talk? I have some ideas to run by you. When should we get together?

Jenny put the phone on the counter, but Liz didn't pick it back up. "Aren't you going to answer him?"

"No. I'll let him stew about it."

"What does Tyler have to stew about? He wants to talk. That's not hard." Jenny looked at Liz doubtfully.

Liz rolled her eyes. She had thought more of Kyle stewing than Tyler. Kyle couldn't expect her to drop everything, even if Tyler was trying to provide help. "Fine. Type it for me. I'm in the middle of making a salad. Tell him we can talk."

Sure. What do you want to talk about?

The phone buzzed immediately. "Just read it aloud, and I'll tell you what to answer," Liz said as she chopped a cucumber.

Wait. I mean actually talk. Phone or in person?
Sounds serious.

I prefer the vocal kind of talking. Your project needs more attention than texting can offer.

I see. Jenny typed the text for her.

"You're making this hard on him. On purpose," Jenny said.

Another text came in but Liz kept her eyes on the vegetables.

So, phone call?

I'm in the middle of dinner prep with roommates. Now is not good.

When is good? Tonight?

I have a test tomorrow. I'm studying tonight.

You're avoiding me.

No, I have a test.

Jenny giggled as she typed again.

"What are you texting? It doesn't take that long to type five words!" Liz came around the counter and snatched the phone from Jenny. She read the last few texts.

Avoiding you would involve having my roommate carry on this conversation.

So, your roommate is typing for you now?

I'm Jenny. Hi. Liz is furiously making a salad right now.

Liz glared at Jenny. "Finish the salad. I'm taking over."

Jenny laughed and pulled out the carrots.

Hi, Jenny. Thanks. Maybe you can see if Liz is free to talk after her test?

Hi. Jenny is banned from my phone. You're stuck with texting just me.

I'll take it. So after your test?

Maybe...don't you have interviews to do?

During the day. How about tomorrow evening?

Okay. I suppose I could humor you.

I'm a great helper and a fast learner. I already have a few ideas for you.

A wave of emotions filled her. Thoughts of Rick, her ex-fiancé, and the last time she'd let him help with a project swirled around her. He had really wanted to help, too. His agenda to become Kyle's agent had tainted everything he helped with.

She shook her head, wanting to shake the memory of Rick away. This was different. Tyler was different. And she needed the help. Until Kyle found someone else, Tyler was her best chance of getting this project done on time, without having to drop her classes.

She swallowed her pride and typed out one last text. *Can't wait to hear your ideas.*

CHAPTER SIX

On Tuesday afternoon Tyler knocked on the door of Liz's house. A brunette answered and introduced herself.

"Nice to meet you in person, Jenny. I'm Tyler. Is Liz here?"

"Come on in." She opened the door wider to him. "Liz, it's for you."

Liz appeared from a hallway, a hand placed on her cocked hip. She wore tight-fitting jeans and a flared light blue tunic. Her curly hair cascaded down her shoulders and her eyes sparkled beneath long lashes. "Hi."

"Hi."

Liz studied him for a minute. "Are you ready for this? Commit, and there's no going back. I don't have a lot of time to pull this off."

"I'm excited to help. Put me to work."

She squinted her eyes at him, but then nodded, seeming to let some tension in her shoulders go. "Okay."

She motioned him to the couch. A laptop was on the coffee table, flanked by two large stacks of papers. She handed him one.

"This is your homework. It will catch you up to speed on the charity and the projects we have done in the past. We're going for the same feel with our domestic project. It may not get the same attention that we have received for our international projects," she said, twirling a finger in her hair, "but, at this point, it's the best we can do."

"So, the other project can be moved out a year, assuming you get the permits?"

"I hope so. We always create our projects to run in the summer, during the off-season. I spent most of my summer working on the Peruvian school. It'd be a shame if the whole thing fell through completely."

She talked passionately about the charity, and her role in the organization. She pulled up the Happy Moments' website, and clicked through the various photo collections, describing the different things they'd done. Several testimonials of volunteers graced each page, sharing experiences about how serving with Happy Moments contributed to their own happy moments.

It was touching. Tyler was moved by the thoughtfulness of Kyle in putting this organization together and running it in such a lean way that the proceeds were handled with such care. He needed to add more about Happy Moments into Kyle's biography. A section was already dedicated to it, but hearing Liz speak as she gave him a virtual tour on their website excited him even more.

Liz obviously loved the charity. As he listened to her talk about the children she met, and the smiles that she saw as they were presented with very simple toys and candy, admiration welled up inside of him.

An idea started to take shape. "What about doing something with literacy for the project? I know several authors who could donate their time or books and help others. That would be a domestic project."

Liz pursed her lips. "It's not only about giving stuff to others though. It's about serving them. Each year we have hundreds of volunteers who spend their own money to join us in a foreign country to *do* something for others, not just *give* them things. It's more than being a collecting service, it's about providing opportunities for others to serve too. I'm not sure how getting authors to donate extra books would accomplish that."

He nodded slowly. The stack of papers on his lap felt like a boulder, crushing him. "I didn't think about that." It brought out a feeling of regret at not getting involved sooner in causes he felt passionately about. It felt like a switch had been flipped inside of him. He wanted to enjoy the kind of excitement Liz felt from service, not just from donating to a charity, but really making a difference in people's lives with his time.

"That's why this is complicated. It needs to involve more than a few people. And now we have to come up with a domestic destination that makes sense to bring people to. In third-world countries, it's pretty easy to accommodate the sleeping arrangements for volunteers because they are generally sleeping in tents. Here, it's kind of hard to have volunteers fork over money to hotels to be able to serve."

"You've thought through this." She knew what she was doing. She was smart.

"It's what I do. That's why Kyle keeps me around." She said it with a half laugh that gave him pause.

"You're not happy working with Happy Moments?" He watched her closely.

She bit her lip, rubbing it back and forth between her teeth. "Why would you say that?"

His rapt attention concentrated on the perfect shape of her mouth and lips. They were beautiful. Perfectly kissable lips. He blinked back the thought, before he was lost again in the idea of kissing her.

"You looked so excited when you were talking about your actual service with the charity, but when you switched to talking about the organizational side of it," he shrugged. "I don't know, your eyes aren't lighting up like they were when you talked about helping people. You had more spark when you told me about your roommate hiding your keys." He laughed as she glared at him. "Don't worry, your secret is still safe with me."

"The key secret better be safe." She took a deep breath. "Happy Moments is great. It really is. But it's not my dream. It's Kyle's dream. I'm happy to help him, and to be a cheerleader, but this summer was draining. When I finished, I thought I'd have a rush from everything I accomplished. But I didn't have the satisfaction I craved from it. I wanted it to be my dream, and I realized two full summers of Happy Moments is enough. It's not what I want to do."

Tyler nodded. Liz seemed close to Kyle. Why wouldn't she just tell him?

"Please keep that off the record. It would break Kyle's heart to know it isn't my dream."

"I won't tell him." *But you should.*

"Thanks." She tucked a curl behind her ear. She looked like she would say more, but a girl with short, dark hair and a camera around her neck ran into the room. She had a phone up to her ear, dropped a bag next to the front door, and ran out of the room again.

She came back again with a second bag. Her free hand immediately went to her forehead. "Yes. I understand. No. The flu sounds awful. Don't come." She closed her eyes, shaking her head. "Thank you for letting me know. Feel better." She hung up the call. "I hate relying on other people."

"What happened, Coco?" Liz asked.

Coco rubbed her temples. "That's the third person who backed out for my video." Tears welled up in her eyes. "This assignment is turning into a nightmare. The teaser is due tomorrow. I can't film with only twelve people. I'll be docked." Her high-pitched words ran together.

Liz immediately closed her laptop and jumped up to give her friend a hug. "I can help, that's one less person you'll miss." Her voice was soothing.

"Thanks," Coco said.

Liz introduced him to Coco, then asked, "Tyler, want to come help?"

Two minutes ago, solving Happy Moment's problem was all-consuming in Liz's life. But she seemed to turn off that stress and redirect all her energy to her friend. "What about solving your Happy Moments problem?"

Liz raised her eyebrows to him.

She pulled him closer to her, as Coco headed into the kitchen. "I know where my priorities are. But we can try to solve a huge crisis right now, and create a happy moment for someone I care about, or we can spend the entire evening brainstorming possible ideas of ways to help people next year." Liz's curls bobbed up and down as she spoke.

Coco came back with a bottled water, the lines in her brow softened.

He swallowed. He promised Kyle he would make Happy Moments his priority, but that was in reference to him working on the biography. One day wouldn't make too much of a difference either way. The pleading in Liz's eyes captivated him. "I'm in. What do we need to do?"

"How are your acting skills? We're going to be in a movie."

Tyler's heart quickened, and she smiled at him, silently encouraging him to agree to the change in plans. He wasn't an actor, but between keynote addresses and book signings, he was confident he wouldn't embarrass himself. "It just so happens that you are looking at the winner of the eighth grade monologue competition."

Coco let out a small laugh. "Ah. Finally, a true professional." She sniffed. "Liz has only done TV spots, hardly helpful."

Liz laughed. "Hey. I can hold my own."

"Thanks, guys. My other group will be waiting for me. Can you meet at Boulder Creek by the track in twenty? I like the background, but we may head back to the business area if I don't get all my shots. I have all of your props." She handed them several papers. "Here is the general sketch of my video. Your portion is highlighted. It's a silent teaser." She gave Liz another hug. "You're the best. Thanks for helping out with this."

Coco ran out the door, and Liz turned back to Tyler.

"I guess Happy Moments will wait another day?" he asked.

She nodded. "Coco needs this. Thanks for coming along."

"I'll drive. You navigate and read our parts."

"'Never look directly at the camera unless asked to do so. No chewing gum.'"

"Good tips," Tyler said.

"There's more. 'Coco will direct as she films the silent movie. However, please talk normally so the footage looks believable. Fifteen people are required for the large group shot. Each vignette presented in the video must be included in the large group shot.'" She looked up from the paper. "Oh, that's interesting. Everyone has to be together before she breaks them up into smaller groups. No wonder she was stressed about coordinating so many people for this project."

"What exactly are we acting out?" Tyler asked. He wanted to start getting into character. One that would impress Liz rather than embarrass her in front of her roommates. He glanced over at her, and noticed Liz's cheek and neck were red and blotchy.

Liz cleared her throat. "The theme of this video is 'Promise.' Coco must convey a distinct emotional promise from each vignette. Ours is the promise of growing love." Liz kept her eyes on the paper.

The part was simple enough, though Tyler could tell the idea bothered Liz.

"Do you want to call someone else to act with?" He didn't want to make her uncomfortable.

She looked at him. "Do you have a girlfriend?"

"No." Did she care? Or was it just polite to inquire? After all, if they were going to act in love, it'd be helpful to know. That must be it.

"It'll be fine."

They joined the group Coco assembled, and followed the directions she gave about slowly moving from one spot to another. They acted out their individual pieces while Coco filmed everyone in the group shot.

Coco took the vignettes separately, going into more detail with each part. It was fascinating to watch the way the movie was coming together. It reminded him of writing a book. Outlining it, and getting the rough idea and then delving into the individual chapters. A woman sporting a blond bob came toward them.

"You must be Tyler. Hi. I'm Mandy, one of Liz's roommates." She smiled brightly at him.

He had noticed her during the whole vignette. She sat on a rock next to where Tyler and Liz sat on a bench.

"Nice to meet you, Mandy." He shook her hand. "What is your part in the vignette? I saw you drawing."

"It's the promise of completion. Thankfully Coco gave me enough time to create the same drawing four times." She showed him her sketchbook. "Each time she comes by, I flip to the next page, and pretend I'm in the middle of the project. The last time she comes by, I'm going to have the pencil on the completed drawing. During the follow-up shoot in a few weeks I will display the drawing in a frame."

The completed sketch was professional enough to be on a book cover. Her style and shading, even as a quick sketch displayed her expertise. "You're very talented."

"Thanks." Mandy turned at Coco calling her over for her vignette.

Liz leaned over to Tyler. "No worries if you can't make the follow-up shoot. We can always find someone else, and put them in sunglasses, or shoot in from a distance."

Tyler put his arm around Liz, the way Coco wanted it in their first shot. "Trying to get rid of me? I'm still here for a few weeks."

Liz laughed. "Yes. You are. And you committed to help me with Happy Moments, so I'm holding you to that."

Tyler watched Coco film the vignette of Mandy and then another one where a boy held up a small umbrella.

"Coco's very talented at filming, isn't she? She's very creative."

"She is." Liz raised her eyebrows. "Did you want me to set you up with her?"

Tyler shook his head. "No. She's not my type."

"Good news. Because it wouldn't work anyway. She has a long-distance relationship with a guy."

Why did Liz ask about setting him up with Coco? Especially when Coco was unavailable? Was she testing him? Or curious?

Coco motioned for Liz and Tyler to take their places on a bench. They each started at opposite ends and slowly moved closer until they sat next to each other.

He knew from the logical part in his brain that he and Liz were simply playing a part for Coco's movie. But as he took her hand, and they strolled down the curved sidewalk, it felt more real than pretend.

Coco followed behind them, giving directions as they continued. "Keep holding hands, that's it. Let's reset this shot again, but I'm going to get it from the front this time, so I can splice the video together."

They went back to the bench, going through the same motions again, with Coco filming from a different angle.

"Got it. This time I need more expression in your face. The beginning is fine to not talk, but when you're next to each other, I need some conversation." Coco put the camera up to her eye. "I'm rolling."

Tyler looked at Liz. His mind went blank to everything except her eyes, and her full lips. "What should we talk about?"

Liz laughed. "It feels funny knowing that whatever we say is on film."

Coco came toward them, letting the camera dangle around her neck. She placed a hand on her cocked hip. "You guys are pretty obvious. I can totally read lips, and I know that you're not having a *love* conversation. I need something that conveys a promise of love. Try again."

Tyler smiled at Coco's no-nonsense attitude.

Liz blushed and she whispered, "I don't want to repeat this over and over again. Think you can pretend to find me attractive for the next ten minutes?"

"You're the girl of my dreams," he said, squeezing her hand. Sparks flew between them. She studied their entwined fingers while he rubbed the back of her hand with his thumb, enjoying the feel of her smooth skin.

"That'll work." She moved to her side of the bench, holding her starting pose.

Tyler moved to his starting position, wondering if she felt anything when their hands connected. He caught the chemistry.

"And rolling," Coco said, then continued to give them directions. She commented on their facial expressions and how soon to move closer to each other.

First, he moved on the bench. Liz followed. After Tyler slid over again, they both looked at each other and smiled. Then Liz moved over, leaving her hand next to her leg. She looked in the opposite direction of Tyler. He scooted closer still, covering her hand with his. He put his arm around her, and noticed that she shivered under his touch. He brushed it off. They were both acting.

She leaned toward him, and he caught the faint smell of coconut from her hair. The hand he had on her shoulder instinctively moved up to touch her curls. They were soft. She glanced up from where she nestled into his shoulder. He turned slightly toward her, his fingers still playing with her hair. Her hazel eyes had flecks of gold in them. They caught the light, making her eyes appear the color of caramel.

Time and space and everyone around them seemed to escape his mind as he drew closer. Her lips were so close to his. The connection he felt with her seemed to grow stronger as he maintained eye contact. Her eyebrows rose and he noticed her lips.

"And cut," Coco announced.

The words seemed to break the spell they were both under, and Liz quickly moved away. Her breathing was as rapid as his own. Would she have let him kiss her if Coco hadn't said anything? The memory played in his mind through the rest of the shoot.

"Now I'm going to film from over here, but I'm zoomed in on you. Take it from your final pose on the bench, and then stroll toward me."

The smell of coconut intoxicated him, as he tried to keep his mind on walking in a straight path toward Coco.

Liz squeezed his hand, and he looked at her, wishing this moment was real.

He squeezed her hand back, noticing how she was the right height to have their hands perfectly in sync together.

They did the final scene a few times, with Coco filming from various angles.

"Okay. This is the final shot," Coco said, moving them to a place in the path framed by large trees. "I'll be fading this final shot, but I want you to get as close as you can to kissing. Foreheads together, noses touching. Something that suggests that there is a promise of love. The promise is what I'm going for. I'll fade before you actually would kiss."

Tyler was about to say it was a shame they wouldn't have to kiss. He could feel the connection between them, but Liz spoke first.

She talked through a gritted smile. "Coco is going to get an earful for this. I'm really sorry. We should have stayed working on Happy Moments. One take to get this over with?"

He exhaled, feeling deflated. She didn't feel the same way. It made sense. They just met. They were a stand-in for the people who canceled, likely an actual couple. "Sure," he mustered. He followed Coco's instructions, placing his hands around Liz's waist, but didn't look her in the eyes, afraid they'd betray his growing attraction for her.

He ignored Liz's fingers running up and down his neck as he leaned forward to put his forehead against hers.

She gave a hesitant smile, and tilted her chin up slightly. She was only a breath away.

Tyler held his breath, trying hard not to think about how close they stood.

"How long should we hold this pose?" she whispered.

"Until Coco says cut, I guess," he replied in her ear.

He dared a glance toward the camera, knowing they would have to redo the scene if he broke the fourth wall. Coco stood where she'd been filming. Her camera was around her neck, a grin on her face.

"Are we done?" he asked.

"I'm done filming, if that's what you mean. But since I called cut two minutes ago, you two love birds haven't moved, so I suppose you should finish up." Her eyes sparkled.

Liz glared at Coco. "We're done here."

He was helping Liz help her roommate. That was it. He shoved down his other feelings to evaluate later. He needed to finish planning Happy Moments with Liz so he could get back to working on Kyle's biography. That was why he was here. He almost convinced himself there was something more between them.

Coco came up to them. "Nice work you two. I know I dragged you into this last minute, so if you can't come for the follow-up shoot in three weeks, I understand. Thanks for helping me today."

"I should be able to make it." He glanced at Liz. "Have Liz let me know when it is."

CHAPTER SEVEN

The Happy Moments planning weighed heavily on Liz. She needed to figure out next summer's project soon. And she also needed to focus on *True Story*. The internship was within her grasp. They liked her writing style, and she was still in the application process. They needed to know if she could pull off a compelling story on a deadline. One of *True Story's* mantras was when there is a story, you make time for it now.

She stared at her inbox, again, willing the e-mail from *True Story* to pop up. *True Story* wanted an article within twenty-four hours of e-mailing their topic out. She'd written pieces that fast before. But they didn't give her an indication of when the e-mail would come or what the topic would be. No new messages. She wanted it to come today. She had a little more time before meeting with Tyler tonight to go over Happy Moments.

Tyler. The memory of helping Coco replayed in Liz's

head every spare minute she had. Amidst school and work and texting back and forth with Tyler on ideas for Happy Moments, Tyler's smile captured her entire senses.

She was being silly, of course. She wasn't going to fall for someone who wanted to work for her brother. She'd done that before, and it turned into a broken engagement only days before the wedding. Not that she regretted throwing her ring at Rick's head, but she wouldn't make the same mistake again. She'd find somebody who was unconnected to her family. Maybe someone who didn't follow football obsessively.

Thinking of her almost kiss with Tyler though. That had her wondering, over and over.

"Earth to Liz," Jenny's voice called. "Wow, that must have been some thought."

"Sorry," she said, shaking her head. "I'm trying to figure out...what I'm going to do for the charity project."

Jenny raised her eyebrows, but didn't say anything else.

Coco came running into the room with her laptop. "My individual vignettes are all done. Want to see them?"

"Done already? I thought you only needed to do the group shot this week," Jenny said.

"I turned in the big group teaser today. The individual vignettes aren't due until next week, but last night I had a lot of inspiration. They're done, but if they need a tweak..." her voice trailed off.

Liz nodded. "Hook it up to the TV and let's enjoy it

on the big screen." A distraction was exactly what she needed.

Mandy wandered in from the other room. "Is it movie time? I love Coco's movies. Pause for two minutes and thirty seconds. I'm making popcorn." She went into the kitchen to get the movie snack ready.

Jenny rolled her eyes. "Yuck. Make it four minutes and pop it fresh. No microwave stuff."

Mandy poked her head around the corner of the kitchen. "What's that, Jenny? I can't hear you over the microwave popping it for me."

"At least add some peanut butter M&M's to my bowl to make it taste better."

Mandy held up a bag and shook it. "Got you covered."

They watched a few different vignettes. Mandy drew her picture, and the promise of completion was so clean, and the cuts and fades so well done, it looked like she sat there the whole time drawing and sketching.

"Wow," Mandy said through handfuls of popcorn, "You made me look good."

"That's all you," Coco replied. "You're a natural."

Jenny's vignette was a promise of determination. It cut from Jenny studying to her wearing a cap and gown.

Comments continued through the clips, as they complimented Coco more. Coco's cheeks looked like they might hurt from smiling so much.

She clicked onto another clip. Liz's cheeks heated as she watched herself on screen. She and Tyler moved closer toward each other until they were practically snuggling. She hadn't realized from the outside how intimate the scene looked. They walked away from the camera, holding hands, and her hands tingled. Her breath caught at the memory.

She had to remind herself to breathe. She was wrapped up in the moment, and leaned closer to the screen as Tyler's smile accentuated the dimple in his left cheek. He moved toward her, and she watched herself leaning toward him. She bit her lip, wiggling it between her teeth.

The camera angle sprang from her to him, each time closer to the screen. Had she been so caught up in Tyler she missed Coco getting so close to them? She couldn't say why exactly she felt disappointed when the scene ended just as they looked like they might kiss.

She turned to Coco, stunned. Coco was *good* at getting the audience to engage in the footage, feeling the emotions of the scene like they were actually there. Then again, she had been there. This *was* her.

Coco tilted her head at Liz and Liz wondered if Coco spent the entire clip studying her. The thought unnerved her.

Liz swallowed. "That was a powerful scene."

"You're both good in front of the camera."

Liz smiled. "Yes. We're both great actors."

Coco raised an eyebrow. "I don't know about that."

"We're not? That footage was believable."

"Oh. It's completely believable. It looks like you've got all sorts of feelings for each other." Coco smiled.

Liz blanched, looking to Jenny and Mandy for support.

"Don't look at me," Mandy said to Liz. "Did you see the stars in your eyes? And in his? It's believable. Definitely not emotions that are easy to fake." Her voice was practically a squeal of delight.

"Coco made us do the scene about ten times," Liz said, though she didn't sound convincing to her own ears. There'd been a moment where she thought Tyler would kiss her, but as they finished he hadn't even looked her in the eyes. Just stared in between them at the bridge of her nose. Her roommates were wrong.

"That's right, she did. And every time you seemed to enjoy it more," Jenny said, ribbing Liz a little. "Come on, admit that it isn't the worst idea in the world to think of Tyler as more than just your brother's biographer."

There was no stopping them, except to agree. "Alright. I do think of him as more than Kyle's biographer."

Three pairs of wide eyes met hers.

Jenny nodded approvingly. "See, that wasn't so hard."

"He's also my assistant as I redo my entire summer of planning for Happy Moments," Liz said. "Great job, Coco. I don't think you should change a thing."

Jenny rolled her eyes. "You're impossible, Liz. I want to see it again. Coco, it's time for an encore."

Liz pulled out a notebook. "I better get back to brainstorming about the charity event."

Coco said, "Spill it. Why are you determined not to like Tyler? He seems like a great guy."

Jenny understood her position. Why couldn't Coco and Mandy see it? Sure, they had chemistry, but a relationship that was built because of her family would never work for her. She'd always wonder if she was enough without her family and family name. "I don't like it when people are already connected to my family." But maybe Tyler *was* an exception to the rule. After all, they'd had a flirty conversation before he knew she was related to her family.

"Because they already like him?"

"Because Rick did that. Weaseled his way into my family. He was more interested in being part of my family than marrying me." But the idea felt like an outdated excuse.

"This isn't that same situation," Jenny said.

"Tyler is working for my brother. It's practically the same." Though Tyler wasn't using his connection to Liz to work for her family. He already established his relationship with Kyle before he knew Liz. Still—she should be cautious.

Jenny shook her head. "He's writing a biography for Kyle, not trying to be his agent. It's different."

"But..."

"Besides, if you just met him at a football stadium and spilled a drink on him, wouldn't you be interested in him? Hypothetically speaking of course." Coco moved her mouse across her screen, dragging the timeline marker to the left, pausing on a clip of Tyler and Liz together. Coco patted her arm, gesturing toward the moment that filled the TV screen. "Just a thought for you. Maybe it wouldn't be so bad." She winked at her, leaving the image up, and left the room.

Maybe it wouldn't be so bad? Maybe it would be incredibly amazing. Tingles formed in her fingers as she thought of Tyler. Had she met him under different circumstances, she would have been interested. Who was she kidding, she *was* interested, until she realized he was sitting with her family.

A knock at the door jolted her from the idea. "Tyler," she said, as she opened the door. "Come on in." She turned toward Jenny. Liz needed to get her attention to turn off the screen paused on a close-up of her and Tyler. Awkward.

"I went through all of the paperwork and previous data. I'm up to speed." He looked like he wanted to sit on the couch, where they worked yesterday.

She cleared her throat. "Let's use the kitchen table." She took his arm to keep him turned toward the kitchen. The touch was a mistake, as fireworks zinged through her. She glanced over her shoulder at Jenny who got the message. Coco's laptop screen was no longer projected onto the TV. *Thank you, Jenny.*

Liz pulled out her laptop bag from the corner, and set up her computer at the table. He did the same. Nerves fired off inside of her. She'd just watch them almost kiss in Coco's movie. Her heart raced as his shoulder brushed hers.

"Where do we start?" Tyler asked her.

His voice melted over her like the butter on the popcorn. *Concentrate. On the charity, not those green pools he calls eyes.* She clicked open her old brainstorming ideas from previous sessions with Happy Moments. The list was long.

"This is what I've had from previous meetings. They're all good ideas. But they're all international. They might spark ideas for a domestic project though."

"May I?" he asked, pointing to her mouse.

She nodded, and he leaned forward, scrolling down the page to see the bottom of the list. She took long, slow breaths as he inched closer to her. She kept her eyes focused on the screen, and on the few lines that he highlighted. The scent of his cologne filled her senses. He smelled good.

"These are my favorite ideas." He had highlighted seven projects, ranging from building schools, to helping with sanitary water for villages, to conservation gardening.

"So now, we need to decide if we can make it work on a domestic level," Liz said.

"Trying to do it internationally is out of the question?"

"There's so much research that goes into all of these. Finding locations and gaining permission takes too long. We started brainstorming for the Peruvian school project last year."

Tyler whistled. "We really have our work cut out for us, don't we?"

We. It was such a small word. But it sounded nice. "Yes, we do."

They spent the next two hours brainstorming

different ideas and states to hold the service project. Then they researched other charities, finding out what their current reaches were in certain areas. They wanted to find the right niche. Liz made a note to call the dwindling Happy Moments staff in Dallas tomorrow. Kyle didn't have enough staff to help in the brainstorming section of his charity, but at least one person there should be able to answer a few questions she and Tyler came across.

Since she dealt almost exclusively with the international politics, she wanted to get a handle on the scope they could have for a domestic project. Housing people during a service project was one of the top barriers. She didn't want people staying at expensive hotels while they donated their time and their money to help with whatever project they were trying to do. It wasn't how they'd done things in the past.

Tyler shouldered his laptop bag. "I'd better get going. I have an early start with Grip tomorrow. I'm shadowing him all day. Practices are early."

"Thanks for your help today. You don't have to do this, but I'm really grateful you agreed to help."

The intense look he gave her made her shiver. "I'm glad to help. We'll get there." He gave her a smile that revealed his dimple, making her slightly weak in the knees. He paused by the door. "What are you doing tomorrow night?"

"Thursday? Every spare minute I have until the charity dinner is planned, I'm working on this." She acknowledged the table overflowing with paper.

"Right. Of course. Want me to come help again?"

Her pulse quickened. She wished she wouldn't have put the charity out there so quickly. Maybe he wanted to ask her out. But she had to get the service project planned. As fun as it was being around Tyler, she couldn't lose her focus. "Sure. That'd be great."

"Okay. I'll call you when I'm done shadowing Grip," he said. "Good night."

He opened the door to leave, and Coco came into the room. "Tyler! Hi. I didn't know you were coming over. What did you think of the movie clip?"

"The movie clip?" He scrunched his eyebrows together.

"He has to go," Liz said, shooting Coco a look.

"It's less than six minutes. Would you like to see it?"

He eyed Liz for a moment before smiling at Coco. "I'd love to see what you did."

Liz resigned herself to the butterflies that she knew would ascend her stomach during the vignettes. Maybe she should go and do something in the kitchen and avoid it. That was silly. She was making too big of a deal out of this.

She sat first, and Tyler sat close to her. Not so close that they were touching, but close.

Liz focused on the first vignettes. She noticed things she hadn't seen the first time. Coco's brilliance of movement and timing with the music and the fades was artistic.

Tyler gave commentary through each one, and Coco would ask questions about the feel and mood of each vignette. His answers were thoughtful and Coco seemed to appreciate the feedback.

As the vignette of Liz and Tyler started, Liz stole a sideways glance at him. He stopped giving commentary to Coco in the middle of the clip. He just watched it. Liz wished he would say something.

It ended. Tyler still gazed straight ahead of him. The suspense made Liz's heart race again.

Finally, Coco broke the silence. "So?"

Tyler shook his head, then grinned at her. "You're very talented, Coco. I really liked it. Good luck on your assignment."

"Thanks. I'm glad you liked it. I'll let you guys know when I need to do the sequel." She unplugged her laptop, and floated out of the room.

Liz felt awkward. He'd complimented the camera angles, and the acting, and the timing and the music choice. But he hadn't said anything during theirs. She wished he had left before Coco came into the room. She stood up and he followed her lead.

"Thanks again for helping with the movie. And with the charity, too." Liz walked him to the door. "Coco was really happy how it turned out, so I guess that's what really matters." Her words tumbled out of her mouth, filling every crevice of silence between them. "See you tomorrow?"

Tyler looked at her lips. Was he thinking about their almost kiss too? He opened his mouth, then shut it again. Finally, he said, "Sure. Great. Tomorrow. After I shadow Grip."

Liz opened the door for him. "I'm looking forward to it. I mean, to planning the charity tomorrow with you." The words felt hot in her mouth.

He smiled at her, turning the inside of her to mush. "Bye, Liz."

"Bye." Liz closed the door behind him, and leaned against it. Her pulse was erratic. She closed her eyes and tried to steady her breathing, but it seemed Tyler took the ability with him when he left. Watching an almost kissing scene with the person she almost kissed, would do that.

Tyler and her almost kiss swirled in her brain the rest of the night. It was going to be hard to concentrate on the service project around him.

CHAPTER EIGHT

Tyler ate his breakfast the next morning at the kitchen island. He was staying with his sister, Stephanie, and her husband Jim, while he was in town. His small room looked much the same as it had growing up. They'd updated a few rooms in the house, but mostly it was old and full of memories.

They lived close to the CU campus, where Jim taught in the English Department, and Cassie lived at home to save money. Stephanie taught high school biology. The only time their schedules all seemed to intersect was in the mornings. Early. Tyler hoped he'd be able to see everyone before he left to shadow Grip.

He wrote notes down in his notebook, as he ate his eggs, trying to wrap his brain around Kyle's biography, and shadowing Grip today. Grip's schedule was similar to what Kyle's had been. Though Tyler had most of the information in journals and other articles, he wanted to experience first-hand what a typical day for an up and coming sports star felt like, before he made it to the NFL.

It was a good angle, if he could stay focused. His mind kept wandering back to last night—to helping Liz on the charity project planning. But mostly it was on the movie Coco had shown him. The scene with him and Liz together, acting like they were in love caught him off guard.

He hadn't dated anyone seriously in the last few years. Sure. He'd gone on dates. And there was always a promotional book launch party to host or attend, where he would bring a date. But this felt different. So different.

He couldn't get the right words out after watching himself on the screen. He knew they hadn't kissed during the filming. But that didn't compute the way Coco had put the footage together. He really thought they were going to kiss. Actually kiss. It was like a well-crafted scene in his novels, driving the reader to pick up on the clues. Laying out all of the evidence, and increasing the expectation of the reader. And then, it was over. Just the expectation of something, and then a fade to black.

He ran his fingers through his hair. Watching it had left him speechless. That was saying something for an author who lived by the words he could string together. Words were never a problem for him. Until last night. He'd almost grabbed Liz's fidgeting hands and kissed her on the couch. *That's how it's supposed to end.* But he didn't. Instead, he couldn't say two coherent words together.

What would he have said to her? He still wasn't sure.

Since the day they met at the football stadium, she intrigued him.

"She's a puzzle," he muttered to himself. One that he wanted to figure out.

"She? I thought you were working on a biography about a 'he.'" Jim stood at the fridge. How long had he been there? And how long had Tyler been talking to himself?

"It is," he said. It was moments like these when he wished Jim felt more like a brother than a father. And Cassie felt more like a little sister, than his four older sisters ever did.

Watching Kyle's family for the last week opened up old wounds. He loved his family. They were great. It was a small, close-knit group. But there were memories that he missed out on. Memories he could see the Montgomery family living.

Cassie came into the kitchen and started making herself a smoothie. "Good morning, Dad. Hi, Tyler. How did the charity project planning with Liz go last night?"

"It was good. It's a lot of work. We're still brainstorming about a new project," Tyler said.

Jim gave him a questioning look. "Liz?"

He might as well tell him everything. "Liz Montgomery. She's Kyle's younger sister. The big charity event for Kyle's charity Happy Moments, fell through. Liz has to have new plans in place before Thanksgiving so they can be announced at this fancy party Kyle throws every year. I offered to help her with it."

"You have time for that in between writing Kyle's

biography, and interviews?" He raised his eyebrows like a concerned parent.

"I'm making time for it. It's working so far," he said. He finished his breakfast, and packed up his bag.

"Who are you interviewing today?" Cassie asked.

"I'm shadowing Grip. I need to meet him at practice."

"Are you on campus all day with him?" She glanced to her dad, then looked down, her face reddening as she continued to drink her smoothie.

"I think we'll be there most of the day."

"Oh. Well, maybe if there's time we can meet up later for lunch or something." She blushed. "I haven't seen you since we went to Kyle's game on Sunday."

A twinge of guilt crept inside Tyler at mention of Sunday's game, as he realized he loved the bustling of the big family life. The craziness that accompanied the loud dinners and the games and sports they played outside. His growing up hadn't been like that. "I'd like that."

"Have fun," Jim said, over the top of the essays he graded. "Let's plan on a family game night this weekend."

"Sounds good."

Grip clasped hands with Tyler, pulling him into a one-armed back-slapping hug. "Glad you could make it."

"Thanks again for letting me shadow you," Tyler said.

Grip waved his hand in the air. "No problem. Happy to give you a glimpse inside the life of college football."

He handed Tyler a piece of paper. Grip's schedule. "I follow this. In addition to the team practice, I train at the gym. Then I usually go for a run in the evening. You can join me for any or all of it. I don't usually talk during my workouts, but I can answer your questions."

Tyler scribbled a few notes down, absorbing everything Grip said as they went into practice.

"Hey, are you coming over for dinner on Sunday?" Grip asked.

"I think I have plans with my family that night," Tyler said.

"Well, next time you come for dinner, you should bring Cassie with you."

Tyler's eyebrows shot up. Was Grip too shy to ask Cassie out? It seemed ironic that a tough football guy would get tongue-tied around his shy niece. He must be reading too much into it. Grip was a nice guy, making sure everyone was included. That must be it. "I'll let her know she's invited."

Grip ran a hand through his hair. "Thanks. That's great."

The day flew by, and mostly Tyler took notes as he shadowed Grip, and his mind wandered to Liz. He'd wanted to ask her out on a date for tonight. But he understood her need to get the charity service project planned.

Toward the end of the day, they went to the University Memorial Center. Grip pulled out a few books from his bag. "This is where I hang out, and catch up on studying. When the weather is nice I like the outdoors, and sitting by the fountain. But inside is good too." Grip opened a book. "Not that I'm actually going to study right now. I thought I'd give you a taste of what me pretending to study looks like. Not that it's my biography." Grip laughed.

"You've pretty much nailed all of Kyle's major points in his college schedule. It's like you're actually related to him."

Grip's eyes smiled. "I'll take that as a compliment. I love my brothers. And I especially look up to Kyle. He's the reason I'm doing what I'm doing. I want to be like him."

Tyler leaned forward. "That's a nice sentiment."

"You can quote me on it."

"How did Kyle specifically inspire you?" Tyler turned the pen in his hand.

"After Ron got hurt, I was nervous about playing football. I saw the toll it took on Ron, and I didn't want to end a football career early. Sam decided to go into sports medicine shortly after that. And at the time, I thought it was because of Ron's injury.

"But Kyle said that fear of injury was not a reason not to live my dream. As long as I wasn't being reckless and stupid, I should pursue whatever it was I wanted in life."

Grip stared past Tyler, seeming to look into the distant past before meeting his gaze once again. "It's moments like that when it matters who the advice comes from. My parents have always been supportive, but I don't think the same words from my dad would have created the same feelings in me. My dad was also my coach. He wanted to see me succeed. And I already knew what success meant in his eyes. But Kyle. Kyle didn't have to say anything, and yet, he did. And it made a difference."

Kyle had certainly played a major role in Grip's defining moment. That spoke volumes about Kyle's character. Grip taking stock in Kyle's advice, and moving past his fear was no small feat. Tyler wanted to ask more. "So, tell me—"

Cassie came and stood by the table. "I'm sorry I couldn't get lunch with you. Any chance we can do dinner?"

Grip and Tyler both said hello at the same time.

"Hi, Grip. It's good to see you."

"It's good to see you too." Grip's cheeks reddened in a blotchy pattern the same way Liz's had.

She bit her lip, then turned to Tyler. "So, dinner?"

Before Tyler could respond, Grip jumped in. "Tyler has plans tonight with Liz. But I'd love to take you out for dinner."

Cassie looked between both of them, finally settling her gaze on Grip. "I'd like that. Thanks." How was this so easy for Grip and Cassie, when he couldn't get the words out with Liz?

CHAPTER NINE

Tyler stood in line at the Purple Apple restaurant. He let another couple go in front of him. He still wasn't sure what to order. He had texted Grip a picture of the menu, asking for his advice on what Liz might like to eat, since he decided to pick up some food on the way to her house. Grip still hadn't replied.

Maybe he should just text Liz the menu and have her choose for herself. Or maybe she'd already eaten. A full day with Grip was enough to make Tyler buy one of everything in the restaurant. Grip had mentioned that he and Liz liked to eat at this eclectic soup and sandwich shop.

His phone buzzed in his hand. Grip texted back. *Liz always gets the number seven combo. She likes the caramel filled cookie. Water with lime on the side.*

He stepped back into line and texted back a thanks.

He knocked at Liz's door, unsure why the food bag

felt slippery in his hand. The last time he stood here visions of kissing Liz filled his senses, rendering him speechless. What he really wanted to do was take her out for a nice dinner. On an actual date.

But she made it clear yesterday that her priority was getting the service project planned, so he hadn't asked her. He looked down at the bag. Was bringing food unannounced okay? If they were in New York, he knew exactly which bistro they would have gone to, to discuss the charity. The seating was limited, but the food was so good.

Coco opened the door. "Come on in, Tyler. I'll go get Liz."

Tyler went into the kitchen and set up on the table. He put her turkey avocado sandwich and tomato basil soup combo meal in front of where she sat yesterday, then took his out of the bag. He finished arranging the napkins and plastic utensils on both sides of the to-go boxes, just as Liz walked into the room.

"What's all this?" She gestured to the table.

"Dinner. Thought we should have some before we work on the project."

"The Purple Apple is one of my favorite places around here. I love their number seven combo." She opened the box. "This is the seven. Lucky guess?"

"Grip may have helped me with the details," he said grinning sheepishly.

"Ah, see. Sometimes twins have their advantages," she said teasingly. "Thank you."

"You're welcome," he said. "Shall we?" He stood by

her chair and held it out for her, then slid her chair carefully in.

Her face went slightly red. "Thank you."

"How was your day?" he asked.

"It was good. My boss was in a meeting when I left, so I didn't have to work late. How did shadowing Grip go?"

"It was fun. He is really dedicated to football." Their whole family was, and Tyler could see the pressure Grip was under to follow the prescribed dream.

Liz nodded. "We all are. It's in our blood. Grip looks up to Kyle a lot. When Grip and I started college, Kyle walked Grip through how he succeeded. Grip has followed the plan exactly. He hopes to catch the eye of recruiters this year."

"That's great." With Grip's determination, and following Kyle's advice, Tyler had no doubt that Grip would succeed.

Liz unwrapped her sandwich. "Thanks. I hadn't thought about dinner yet."

"Next time we can do something fancier," he said between bites.

She arched an eyebrow. "Next time?"

That was presumptuous of him. Who was to say there would be a next time, or that she would want a next time. "I mean, uh..." It was impossibly unfair that his mind couldn't work around her.

Her lips quirked, drawing his attention to them, and flooding his mind with memories of watching them pretend to be in love. *Pretend.* That was the operative word. He wasn't in love. But he was intrigued.

She bumped his shoulder. "Just giving you a hard time. I'm sure we'll be at this for quite a few next times." She smiled at him, and then ate another bite.

"I was thinking maybe the service project should be in Texas," she said, once she finished her food.

"Why Texas?" he asked, clearing their to-go boxes into the bag they came in.

She shrugged. "It's where Happy Moments' headquarters are, so it might be easier to organize from there." She played with the end of her ringlets, and he was lost in the softness of her curls.

"That's a valid point. Any thoughts on what you'd want to do?" he asked.

"That's just it. There are lots of things we could do everywhere. It's trying to find the match between how many we expect to show up and what we can actually accomplish in a weekend of service. I can't think that we'll be able to keep people for a whole week on a domestic project."

"What about helping an elementary school that needs a new playground? Or finding a park that needs some work on restoring benches or landscaping paths or something?"

"Those could work," she said slowly. "I have a few leads." She pulled up a map. "This is an older park that is run down, but could be really nice with some care."

"Is it the kind of thing Happy Moments would want to do?" Tyler asked.

"Maybe," Liz said. "I'll be sure to ask Kyle and a few people at Happy Moments if helping with this park would make an impact on the community, or what the plan for renovation is with the city."

Happy Moments had mailed Liz packets containing project proposals put together by organizations and cities soliciting help. They each took a pile, and began looking through them. Some were outdated. Others didn't fit their time frame. Liz was insistent that the service take place in the summer. That ruled out going to certain states, like Arizona.

"We can always find the location first and then ask the city for suggestions."

"I'm open to the idea." Liz grinned at him, then looked away, typing at her computer. She sighed. "I have nothing promising in this stack. You?"

"Not domestic ones, but there are a lot of international opportunities."

"They'll be great options for future years."

After two hours of working through the files they still weren't through the entire stack. It wasn't late, but they were both hitting a wall. "Should I come back Saturday afternoon to finish the rest of this? I'm shadowing your dad tomorrow at the high school, and tomorrow night is their first home game," Tyler said.

"Saturday is also CU's home game."

"Yes."

"So, I'm watching the game."

"Kyle lets you take off for that sort of thing, does he?" he teased.

Liz flashed him a smile, and he was mesmerized by her full lips again, and the coconut scent that filled her hair. "I take my cheering responsibilities seriously. If Grip is playing, I'm watching."

"Unless you're trying to avoid your brother setting you up, of course."

She laughed. "Of course. I take my football seriously. And I also seriously avoid being set up."

"Sounds like you've got a story behind that." He wondered if she would share it.

She chewed on her lip. It was a sign Tyler recognized in her when she became uncomfortable. He hoped he hadn't pushed her too far. She pursed her lips together, and he thought she might never tell him, but she surprised him.

"I was engaged a few years ago. Rick was a guy Sam introduced me too. At first, he was nice and attentive. I mean, there were enough sparks that we were engaged. I liked that he wanted to be around my family. We were always with one of them. He seemed to really hit it off with everyone."

"What happened?" He scooted closer to her.

"As it turned out, he wanted to marry into my family, more than he wanted to marry me. His plan was to become Kyle's agent once we were married. He had this preconceived idea that if he was family, he'd make a bigger percentage." She brushed at her shirt sleeve.

"But you found out beforehand?" The whole situation had his stomach in knots for her.

She nodded. "Thankfully yes. Grip figured it out,

and called him on it. He got defensive but tried to backpedal. Then Kyle let Rick know he wasn't going to be switching agents. Rick got super mad. My brothers and dad escorted him out of the house, and I threw my ring at his head."

He couldn't think of anything to say. The guy had been a jerk, but she already knew that. No wonder she was cautious in her personal life. "Ouch."

"It left a nice purple bruise." She smiled, satisfied.

"I meant about the whole thing. Finding out you're being used for your connections. That's gotta be tough."

"The worst kind of betrayal."

He didn't know what to say. It would all sound hollow. But he was beginning to understand her better. "You don't want to be used for your connections in your own family. It makes sense."

She shuffled her stack of paper on her lap. "We're way off topic."

"And you don't want your brothers setting you up anymore."

She shook her head. "They don't usually offer at this point." She pointed between them. "And obviously, Sam wasn't trying to set me up, as it turns out. He wanted to introduce me to the biographer." She bumped his shoulder with her own.

"I guess it's good that he didn't set us up. I might still have a chance."

Her laugh sounded nervous. Maybe he misread the way she bantered with him through the last few times they'd been together. "I stay away from anyone who works with my family too. It keeps me safe."

"My loss," he muttered before he had time to think about saying the words aloud.

"Yeah, right."

"Serious. And technically, we had chemistry before you knew I was the person you were supposed to be introduced to."

"Is that so?"

"You told me the secret about your roommate hiding your keys."

She smiled. "I did say that, didn't I?"

"If I had asked for your number that day?"

"You didn't though."

"My mistake again. Would you have given it to me?"

"Yes."

He took the plunge. "Perhaps we can remedy that situation."

She raised her eyebrows. "You already have my number."

"Can we go on an actual date? For real food." Was it too forward right after she spilled her whole relationship saga to him?

"You brought me fake food today?" Her eyes sparkled.

He wanted to get to know her beyond the stress of Happy Moments, and interviewing her. "I mean food you eat at a restaurant with actual silverware, not plastic utensils."

"Sounds fancy."

"That sounds like a yes."

She gave a half shoulder shrug. "I mean, I like eating real food."

"Saturday night?"

"I'll be hungry."

Both of the phones buzzed at the same time. "Strange coincidence," he said, "Do you mind if I check it?"

"Go right ahead. I'll do the same."

He read the message. "It's Cassie. She's out with Grip, and is wondering if we'll come join them bowling."

"Moral support?"

"I'm guessing it's not to chaperone."

"Grip said it would be nice if we both came to bowl with him. That's not like him."

"Asking you to double?"

"No. Bowling before a game. That's the activity of choice after he loses a game."

Or maybe Cassie chose the activity. "Should we join them?" he asked.

Liz looked around at the stacks they'd made. "I think my brain is fried on potential service projects for one night. Let's go."

It wasn't an official date, but he'd spend any time he could with her. "I'll drive."

CHAPTER TEN

Tyler and Liz found Grip and Cassie on the center lane of the bowling alley.

Cassie ran and gave Tyler a hug when she saw them approach. "I'm so glad you made it. We're ready to start." She looked between the two of them and smiled. He wondered if Cassie caught on that he liked Liz.

"Are you guys hungry? We ordered some snacks," Cassie said, motioning to the table.

"Tyler picked up dinner for us," Liz said.

"That was ages ago," Cassie said, motioning to the food.

Grip finished typing in names at the computer, and gave Liz a hug.

"Hey, don't let bowling before a big game jinx you." she said.

"It feels that way though, doesn't it?" Grip responded.

"You'll have scouts fighting over you soon," she said.

"Thanks, Liz."

Cassie and Grip took their turns.

Tyler couldn't take his eyes off Liz.

She picked up her ball and stood on the brown arrows, lining up her ball with the pins. She tested the weight of the ball a few times, then took a few steps forward and released the ball. It rolled straight until half way down the lane and then it curved and headed toward the gutter.

Tyler caught her rolling her eyes as she waited for the ball to come back up. She took a deep breath and reset, taking a step to the left of where she stood before. This time the ball made contact with the pins. Seven pins down.

"Better than a gutter ball."

Tyler gave her hand a quick squeeze as she passed by him. He took his ball, wishing he had brought his own. The weight of this ball was lighter than what he was used to. His hands found the holes, and he lined up. His first ball hugged the right side of the lane, teasing the gutter before swinging back to knock over two pins. He opened and closed his fists as he waited for the ball to return. His second ball knocked down six. Grand total of eight.

Tyler took a seat next to Liz. Cassie quirked an eyebrow at him, but Tyler shrugged. He was a little rusty, especially with a light bowling ball. He'd find his game though. Liz's family had football down, but Tyler and Cassie were bowlers.

Cassie picked up her bright pink ball and swung hard.

The crashing sound of the pins triggered the lights and the screen to play a cartoon indicating a strike.

Liz sucked in a breath. "She's good."

"She is," Tyler said. A flare of wanting to impress Liz swelled inside of him. Cassie was a good bowler, but they were evenly matched.

Grip gave Cassie a high five and she gave him encouragement on his bowling.

Grip's pins went down, and he got a spare. Cassie returned the high five and they sat together chatting only to each other.

Liz leaned forward and Tyler caught the scent of coconut. She was so close to him.

She whispered, "We go bowling after a loss so he can win at something. Then we celebrate with ice cream. I've learned to play easy on him for the first few frames, you know, to bolster his confidence. Of course, it's weird playing before a game. I'm still trying to create my new strategy for that."

He squeezed her hand, and though she looked down with wide eyes, she didn't pull away until Grip's voice shattered the moment. "Earth to Elizabeth. Your turn."

She slugged her brother on the shoulder and picked up her bowling ball. Red with yellow streaks swirled in it. It looked like a fireball. He smiled. It fit her well.

She knocked down nine pins on her first try. But the next throw missed its mark by a few inches. He realized her genius in looking like she tried hard to play, though she purposefully threw the first few frames. He wanted to play against her when she didn't hold back.

She tapped him on the knee, and waved her hand in front of his face. "Your turn, sport."

He stood up. "Sport?"

She shrugged but smiled.

Sport? He would show her some sport. He grinned as he aimed his ball toward the pins. Liz wasn't the only one with a bowling secret. He threw his last frame to not get too far ahead of her.

Strikes counted extra points. Too many of those at the beginning and he'd have to try hard to keep his score below 280. He'd done it before, but after hitting seven or eight strikes in a row, it was hard to make two or three frames of gutter balls look convincing.

Tyler put just enough spin on it to send the ball in a twirling motion, but it didn't curve. It spun perfectly down the middle, colliding with the front pins, instantly sending the lights and small cartoon across the screen, announcing his strike.

Cassie, who was ready with her bright pink ball gave him a fist bump.

Tyler sat down as Cassie made her second strike. Liz gave him a high five. "Nice job."

Grip gave Cassie a hug.

"Cassie gets a hug for her strike," Tyler said.

Liz cleared her throat. "The hug came after the second strike, in a row."

Tyler leaned closer. "Three strikes in a row gets a kiss?" His eyes locked on hers. *What did you say?*

"Three strikes and you're out."

"Three strikes in a row is also called a turkey." Smooth. Now he felt really stupid for bringing it up.

"Call yourself a turkey then, if you get that far." Liz laughed as she moved toward the lane for her turn. She took a spare in good spirits.

Tyler paused an extra moment as he studied his ball, placing his hands carefully around it, checking for any rough edges. He couldn't find any. He looked at the pins. Should he knock them all down in one go, or should he play a little easier? He didn't want to steal Cassie's thunder. She was doing well.

She seemed happy with Grip, and that decision settled it for him. He shifted the ball from one hand to the other, and put his right hand in the finger holes. Two pins for the first ball and six for the second one. He sighed. It was only a game. But it was a game he knew he could win. Liz was throwing her game to help Grip, and he could do the same for Cassie, and Liz.

Liz looked disappointed when he took his seat, and he arched an eyebrow at her.

"All that talk and complaints about not getting a hug and kiss for your strikes and you throw something like that?" Liz searched his eyes.

"You sound more disappointed than me." He leaned forward, close enough to take a kiss, and her eyes widened.

"Not what I meant," she said, glancing to the side where Cassie and Grip sat. "Perhaps you're all talk. And you aren't up for a challenge in the game."

His eyes twinkled. "Or maybe I am playing the same game you are." He nodded toward Grip who did a happy dance on his first strike. Cassie gave him a big hug. Each gesture was overdone, but Tyler wished he could have the same type of affection. But not from his niece, of course. From the woman sitting next to him whose eyes were still wide at his admission.

"Your loss."

"Definitely," he murmured.

Tyler blew out a breath. A 180 score. Liz was in the lower 100s, but she seemed to take it in stride. Grip took his second place to Cassie's first, remarkably well. Grip seemed in a fine mood, but maybe that was why he and Cassie had asked Tyler and Liz to join them. Tyler wouldn't hold back in a rematch. "Up for another round?" he asked the group.

Grip and Cassie looked torn, then started speaking together.

"Yeah, get the next game started, we'll go get some food," Grip said.

Small talk took over the conversation as Tyler reentered the names. Several minutes passed and they continued talking, waiting for Grip and Cassie to return. Liz's phone buzzed a few times.

"Do you mind if I text Grip? I'll let him know we switched the order, so we can play."

He nodded, and she unlocked her screen. Her eyes

scanned across the screen as she read a few texts. "Unbelievable," she muttered, then showed Tyler.

Hey, we went to get food, just not at the bowling alley.
Play for us if you already typed in the names. Don't be
mad. Cassie is worried you might be mad. Text me back so
she knows you aren't mad. Have a fun night.

She put her phone down by the computer.

"Aren't you going to answer him back?"

"After I finish deleting Grip and Cassie from the
game." She moved a stray curl from her cheek.

He glanced around. "Normally it wouldn't matter to
me. I mean, he's your brother, but Cassie is worried. She
gets anxious about surprises."

"I hadn't thought of that. I'll send it right now." Liz
typed a quick message, then showed Tyler.

Not mad, but you're about to miss some exciting bowl-
ing. Catch you later. Enjoy your food. Have fun on
your date.

Tyler finished reading the text, just as Grip's
response came in. He read it and chuckled.

Enjoy your date too. :)

"What's funny?" She claimed her phone back, and
read the text.

"You know, I like him, especially when I don't have to
play against him," Tyler mused.

"Ha. That's what most of his buddies say. They like
him. Just not on the field. He's pretty...intense."

Tyler knocked down his second frame with a perfect
strike. Just like the first.

"This is not my game today." Liz looked at the score.

Her first frame was a spare, she needed a strike if she hoped to come close to his score this round.

He grinned as she passed him. "What do I get for a turkey again?" He took in her perfectly white smile, begging to be kissed.

"If we were playing Tic Tac Toe, three X's in a row means you win and the game is over."

"Don't worry, I'll take a rain check. Wouldn't want to get us kicked out for holding up the lane while we kiss."

"Wouldn't that be a sight." She lined up with the arrows down the lane.

"A sight I'd rather experience than see."

She looked behind her, and he caught her grin matching his own. Playfulness in her eyes.

"You're distracting me," she called behind her, then focused back on the pins and released the ball.

"You knocked down nine pins while being distracted? Not bad." Tyler chuckled.

Liz rolled her eyes. "Not fair. I'm talking during your turn to distract you."

"In case you haven't noticed, that's what we have been doing during all of our turns. Talking."

Liz reached for her ball from the return, turning it until she found the three holes, and lifted it from the carousel.

"Yeah, but not about kissing," she mumbled, and lined up again. She knocked over the solitary pin. Another spare. Liz offered a dramatic bow.

"Nice shot," Tyler said. "Those single pin shots always make me nervous. Bravo."

Tyler threw the ball down the alley so fast the collision of his strike reverberated in his ears, crashing again. He turned toward her. "Turkey."

"Yes, you are."

"Now, about my payment." He stepped closer to her, blocking her path to retrieve her bowling ball.

Liz reached up and kissed Tyler on his cheek. "Congratulations."

"A kiss on the cheek isn't quite what I was expecting. You could have done that in our last game without drawing any attention."

"You're right." She kissed him on the other cheek. "Happy?"

"I watched you bowl. Your aim isn't *that* bad. I'll give you one more try to get it right." Tyler spoke low.

Liz hovered her lips close to the cheek she'd first kissed. "Tyler, I think—"

"Hey, we close in ten minutes," a teenaged voice yelled in their direction. "If you're close, you can finish your game. Otherwise, please return your shoes and your bowling balls to the counter."

"We're almost done. We'll clear out within five minutes," Tyler said.

Liz looked doubtfully at him. "We've taken longer than five minutes to bowl a frame or two. We still have three frames to go."

"Let's finish bowling, and talk over dessert," Tyler suggested.

"Okay."

The scores were close at the end of the game, but

Tyler beat Liz. He carried the balls back and she carried their shoes.

"Nice game," she said.

"You too. You gave me a run for my money."

"Hardly."

"It's true. I almost wish you would have won," Tyler said. "But you're cute when you lose."

"Don't let me win." She raised her chin in the air. "That's worse than losing fair and square."

"There's a story behind that, I just know it."

"Alright, spill your story about not winning," Tyler said as they sat down with a dark chocolate cake between them.

"That's not the story." Liz took a corner of the cake off with her fork.

"No?"

"The story is about me not liking when others let me win."

"Ah." He lifted a piece of the cake topped with ganache and whipped cream. "I stand corrected. Proceed."

"Mostly it comes from a memory when I was maybe eight. Ron was already playing college football. We had a family game night around the kitchen table. I can't even remember which one now. But I won. And I gloated, because I had older brothers, and I learned quickly how to act when I won, from them. I guess I was a pretty sore winner."

He smiled back with a teasing glint in his eyes. "I can't imagine that of you."

"Can't you? Perhaps I've grown up since then." She tossed her hair from her shoulder. "I carried on about it all day, and into the next. Must have been a Saturday. We were all watching football together, and I was still rubbing it in their faces that I won.

"Me. Being the only girl, and the youngest, and I won fair and square. Kyle nudged Sam, and said, 'It was definitely a bad idea to let her win.' I was super mad. I jumped up from the couch and wrestled with Kyle.

"Thankfully, my parents had rules about how to wrestle their younger sister, so I had some advantage. I wrestled hard, even pulled some arm hairs."

He laughed as her voice rose in pitch, her fingers mimicking the pulling.

"I told him it wasn't nice to let someone win, and especially not nice if they tell them afterward about it. I pulled on some of his leg hair and wouldn't let go until he promised he would never let me win again. It only took me six months to stop asking every time when I won, if someone let me win."

The way she animatedly shared the memory, changing her voice and acting out the parts of her younger self, and her family, he felt like he had been there. He smiled at the thought of eight-year-old Liz getting upset. Her hair wild as it was now, bouncing up and down as she showed her older brothers their younger sister was a force to be reckoned with.

"You think my story is funny?"

Tyler covered up his smirk with chocolate cake. "I think it's an adorable story. One thing is for sure," he said, grinning as she cocked her head. "I won't let you win a game ever!"

"You're scared of me," she said triumphantly. "I knew it."

In more ways than one. "Guilty. I'd like to keep my arm hair." He wiped his mouth on the linen napkin. The chocolate cake was a good choice over ice cream on a chilly night. And the Italian bistro was open longer than the ice cream parlor anyway.

Liz swirled another forkful of chocolate cake into the ganache, and then daintily savored the bite. Her intense, caramel colored eyes studied him. They were intoxicating.

"So, I'll see you on Saturday," she said, as he walked her to the door.

It was only two days away. Why did that not feel good enough? He had a full load shadowing Jack again tomorrow. The football game would go late. "How about I make us breakfast tomorrow?" he asked.

"A breakfast date and a dinner date?"

"On two separate days. What time is your first class?"

"On Fridays, it's 10:00 a.m."

She looked like she might not take his offer, but he had to see her before Saturday night.

"We can get a head start on more of the charity paperwork."

"We'll get around to that. Breakfast sounds great. What can I make?"

"Nothing. I'll bring it all. 8:30 a.m.?"

She looked like she might let him kiss her, but he didn't want to goad her more after the turkey bowling comments. He wasn't looking for a kiss on the cheek. But then again, she'd told him about Rick earlier tonight. Maybe he was already too connected to her family to have a chance. The thought ran through his mind.

"So, about that turkey," she said, her lips shining under the porch lamp.

He moved closer, giving her a small peck on the cheek. "I got the message."

CHAPTER ELEVEN

L iz tossed and turned in bed all night. Why hadn't Tyler kissed her goodnight? It was one thing not to have their first kiss be at a bowling alley, but on the door step would have been fine, even if it was cliché. She stuffed her face into her pillow. She'd be seeing him twice this weekend just for fun. Dinner was officially a date—not working on her charity event. She didn't want it to be awkward. Ugh.

Breakfast was still over an hour away. That was plenty of time for sundaes for breakfast and a few story swaps. She needed advice on what to do about Tyler. Her roommates would be able to solve the mystery. Between his flirting at bowling, and then his reluctance to kiss her on the doorstep, she was baffled.

She padded out from her bedroom wondering where everyone was and proclaimed loudly to the entire house, "Girls, I need you. My evening last night was unbelievable. It's an ice cream sundae for breakfast kind of morning. I need advice. And lots and lots of caramel."

Liz stopped short when her gaze landed on a pair of bright green eyes. Tyler stood in her kitchen. Did thinking about someone conjure them up?

"What are you doing here?" She pressed a fingernail into her palm to make sure she wasn't dreaming. It wasn't early, but she'd been up half the night thinking about him.

He tilted his head. "We made plans for breakfast, remember?"

She glanced at the clock. 7:20 a.m. "In an hour." Her wild hair and pajamas reflected she had just crawled out of bed.

"I needed to get started earlier to have it ready by 8:30." He smiled. "An unbelievable night?"

She ignored him. "Where are my roommates?"

His smile grew. "I invited them to stay for breakfast. Even told them I had plenty of food, but they scattered without a backward glance. Early classes? Jenny said she didn't want to wake you early since you already knew I was coming over."

Minus the embarrassing moment of announcing her confusion about last night, it was sweet of him to come early to prepare. The table was set and linen napkins were folded into the shape of Peter Pan's boot on both of the plates. She gestured to the tablescape. "I'm impressed."

"I know enough about hosting to not embarrass

myself. Though, I guess it's not really hosting if I'm serving at someone else's house."

"It smells good."

"Hopefully it will be even better when it's finished."

"I'll be right back." She hurried to her bedroom, throwing on some clothes, and running a comb through her hair.

She came back and they chatted, and Liz finally sat on a barstool and put her elbows on the counter after her many attempts at helping Tyler failed. While breakfast baked in the oven, they talked about *True Story*, and Kyle's biography.

The timer went off, signaling it was time for breakfast.

Tyler held out a chair for her, and scooted her in. He brought a large glass dish of baked French toast from the kitchen, and placed it on the table. He'd alternated layers of strawberries and whipped cream between them. Finely shaved chocolate curls sprinkled the artistic structure. He poured some orange juice into her decorative goblets.

"Would you like the ice cream sundae part of your breakfast first?" he asked.

"No. It's a roommate tradition. I'll have my breakfast ice cream sundae tomorrow."

"An odd tradition."

She nodded as she took her first bite of the baked French toast. The strawberries were the perfect complement. "This is delicious. Thanks. Who taught you how to cook?"

"That recipe is my brother-in-law's. Jim is amazing in the kitchen. He enjoys cooking and creating things."

"That sounds great. Growing up in my house, we ate breakfast on the way to an early morning practice. If we ever had pancakes, it was when we had breakfast for dinner, or when we visited my grandparents. And even then, it was from a mix."

"Early morning practice for what?" He ate his food.

She swallowed. "Cheerleading mostly for me."

"But you didn't do that when you were in elementary school, did you?"

"No, I didn't."

"But you still had breakfast in the car?"

"We were always on the run. I practically lived in the car as my mom and dad shuttled my brothers from one football practice to another."

"Was that hard?"

She shrugged. "It was the sacrifice necessary to raise four successful boys in the sport they loved. You don't get two NFL players, with another on his way without some sacrifice." She took another bite.

"Do you have ice cream sundaes for breakfast a lot?"

"As often as we need."

He tilted his head, waiting for more details.

She sighed. "It's something silly Jenny and I started. Freshman year was...character-building for us. It was so full of drama and boyfriends and crazy things that for a while we felt cursed. Anyway, one particular Friday night was just painful. Between the six roommates there was two breakups, one of which was a broken engagement, one stand up, one blind date which turned out to be a third cousin, one proposal, and one flat tire on the side of the road during a rainstorm."

He raised both eyebrows. "All in one night?"

"Yep, we were the over-achieving group when it came to that sort of thing." She smiled at the memory of that crazy day. "As roommates we swapped all the juicy dating stories. I mean, it's not like we kiss and tell." *Stop blushing, Liz. Really.* "But all the good, bad, and ridiculous gets lived at least twice after the actual date." She paused when she noticed him smiling at her and he rolled his index finger in the air for her to continue the story.

"So, anyway, this was one of those unbelievable days where you wouldn't believe it if you didn't live through it. One by one we all came home. It was our tradition to wait until everyone was home to talk about our dates.

"We'd wear our matching sweatshirts and flannel pajama bottoms and swap stories. The rule was you couldn't share anything until everyone was home, otherwise you'd be repeating the story five times."

She took another bite of her French toast and drank the orange juice. The freshly squeezed juice made her mouth pucker. "Did you squeeze this yourself?"

Tyler chuckled. "No. A local store carries it fresh every morning. Do you like it?"

"Love it. It's delicious." She set the glass down and wiped her lips with the napkin. He watched her every movement. She had a sudden desire to spread a little whipped cream on his face.

She pressed her lips together and resumed her

memory. "It was after midnight before everyone arrived home, thanks to the flat tire in the rain fiasco, but usually by one or two a.m. we would be finished with our chatting.

"On this particular night, we started telling our stories at one and we weren't through talking until after six. By that time, we were all exhausted. Normally we'd eat something while we chatted, but every story was so gripping we couldn't pull away from the couch, so finally it was suggested we have ice cream sundaes once we finished.

"By this time it was past six, and one of my roommates was a big runner. But even she broke down and had a bowl of ice cream. It became tradition to tell a quick story at night, then get up on Saturday and have ice cream sundaes to hash through the rest of the details." Liz smiled at the memory and her five original roommates. Freshman year seemed so long ago.

"That's quite a story. And last night was one of those moments? A blind date with a cousin? Or a flat tire in the rain?" Tyler's eyes held amusement.

She had talked herself into a corner. *He* had been with her last night. "Sort of." She measured her words. "Coco has been filming weddings Saturday mornings so she doesn't want to stay up late Friday nights and doesn't have much time on Saturdays. We fill each other in when it works, but not always at the same time, so we still tell stories multiple times."

"Is it hard to keep all of your stories straight?" His lips twitched.

"Maybe a little, but Jenny likes to make lists of them on the fridge so everyone gets a preview or a keyword to remind them which stories they haven't heard yet." She took another sip of orange juice. "It's a little much for me, but Jenny likes to keep up on the list, so it works overall."

He stood abruptly and scanned the paper taped to the fridge.

Liz cringed knowing the words he'd read: root beer and chocolate cake. He glanced back at her, expecting a comment. She had no place to hide.

"I thought this was a shopping list!" He scanned all of the lists. "I guess *gazebo*, *elephant*, and *trumpet*, aren't usually on my grocery list. Yours has all food." He eyed her, and she knew he made the connection to the words and his own involvement in them.

"Well mine usually do, as I am certain to do embarrassing things wherever I go." She bit back the stinging at the admission.

"I don't remember anything embarrassing about the chocolate cake."

"Yes, well, some stories aren't embarrassing." They're moments to remember. *Like watching your dimple when you eat dessert.*

"So, there's a story around chocolate cake? Was I there?"

It had led to their confusing end of the night. Why hadn't he kissed her? She put it on the board so she could analyze it with her roommates. *Maybe you should have kept the list to yourself.* She smiled, shrugged, and finished her breakfast.

He helped clear the dishes from the table. Halfway to the kitchen he stopped. "Speaking of embarrassing moments with food, you have some on your face."

She stopped. "Where?"

He touched her nose, smearing something cold on it. "Right there."

Using one finger she wiped off the whipped cream he'd rubbed on her. "Is it gone?"

He chuckled. "Nope."

Before he could say more she reached up and smeared the whipped cream on his cheek. "Looks like you have the same problem."

He set his dishes down and headed back to the table.

She was rinsing the orange juice out of her goblet when a spoonful of whipped cream hit her on the head.

"Careful there, Tyler. You do *not* mess with these curls. They don't appreciate food."

She lunged for the bowl of whipped cream, but he held it above his head.

He laughed at her attempt to get him back.

She scooped the whipped cream from her hair and smeared it on Tyler's other cheek as he turned, leaving a considerable amount on his jaw and mouth.

Tyler licked his lips, his eyes twinkled. "Delicious. Is that the best you can do?"

"Probably not." She took two steps closer to him, hopped up on the counter, and reached for the bowl.

He held it away from her again, and as he did, she lifted up his elbow, forcing his arm to curve, and used her other hand to tip the bowl onto his head.

They both laughed as whipped cream dripped through his hair and onto the floor. "I didn't see that one coming," he said. He placed the bowl on the counter.

"I win." She grinned at him, removing a huge blob of whipped cream from his hair.

He put his arms at her waist, lifting her off the counter, but didn't let go when her feet touched the floor. He reached a hand up to her cheek, wiping off some whipped cream that had splattered. "I suppose you did." His intense green eyes moved from her eyes to her lips.

Liz gulped in air. Warmth rushed into her cheeks as his fingers lingered on her jaw. She barely drew in a breath before Tyler snatched it from her with a kiss. He held her closer to him, the tenderness melting her.

Liz hadn't been kissed in a long time. A very long time. It was delicious. Tyler was delicious. There were so many moments that swam in front of her, and she ignored them all, just enjoying the sensation. "Maybe it was a tie," she whispered when she resurfaced from Tyler's lips.

He kissed her again, with more passion. "Maybe we should go two out of three. I've never been a fan of ties."

She kissed him gently.

"I'd better get going. I need to run home and shower the whipped cream out of my hair before I shadow Jack today." Tyler's breath came out shallow and ragged.

She felt lightheaded. "Sorry about that." She handed him a small kitchen towel.

"Don't be. I'm not." He pulled her to him one last time.

She drank in one more kiss, before pushing on his

chest. "You'd better hurry. You don't want to be late." Her words raced out uneven as she tried to slow down her breathing. He was going to be with her dad all day, and she didn't want to be the reason Tyler showed up late.

"I'll see you tomorrow night."

"I can't wait," she said. *Especially if there was more kissing involved.* Who needed food? She was hungry for more kissing. When Tyler left she went to the fridge, and wrote *whipped cream* underneath the word *chocolate cake.*

CHAPTER TWELVE

O n Saturday morning clothes were strewn all over Liz's bed and closet floor. She knew she was overreacting. The date with Tyler later tonight wasn't a big deal. Not really. That whipped cream kiss. Why did it keep playing through her head? Now her hair and her stomach were in knots. And everything she tried on ended up on the floor, or the bed.

Jenny came in as Liz examined her outfit—an ivory top with dark jeans. "Oh. That's nice," Jenny said. "What's the occasion? It seems dressy for football."

"Date with Tyler tonight."

Jenny tapped her chin, as if she had solved a puzzle. "That explains the closet exploding all over the floor. Either that or some hurricane tore through here. I could check to see if insurance will cover it."

"Don't bother, the claim won't be able to fix the current problem." She held up another shirt and glanced in the mirror, then threw it on the stack on the bed.

"You're getting really worked up. What's up?"

"He's... the biographer," Liz said, going into her closet again to pull out the next unsuspecting shirt hanging there. "I... want to make a good impression."

"Or those whipped cream kisses are muddling your brain." Her eyes sparkled. "You like him more than I realized."

"I just don't want his opinion of Kyle to be tainted because I picked the wrong shirt."

"Right. Cause that's going to happen." Jenny stepped over to the bed, and pulled out an emerald green shirt Liz had discarded. "This one always makes the golden flecks in your eyes pop. But I like the ivory one you're wearing too."

Liz felt the sleeve of the green shirt. The light material would keep her cool in the sun during the game. She changed shirts then gave her look a critical view in the mirror. With a gold necklace, she could jazz it up for the evening. "This is perfect, Jenny. Thanks for your help."

Jenny looked around the room. "Next time, come get me before you blow in here and destroy everything!"

The doorbell rang. "Are you expecting someone?" Jenny asked.

"Nope. Probably for one of the others," Liz said, holding up a pair of jeans to her shirt.

"The jeans you have on are great. Don't change," Jenny called down the hallway. "Mandy left this morning for another work trip, and Coco is shooting a wedding."

Jenny answered the door, and Liz could hear her talking to someone.

Liz threw on a pair of wedges, and twisted her hair off her neck. Maybe she'd put her hair up tonight.

Jenny's voice wafted to her room. "Lizzy Lou, someone to see you."

Liz hurried to the front door, surprised to see Tyler standing there, talking to Jenny.

Jenny excused herself.

"I thought we were doing dinner tonight," she said.

He was grinning so wide. Liz's breath hitched in her throat. He had a great smile. And those lips. Had he missed her too much to wait to see her until tonight? Giddiness swirled around her.

"I know. But I wanted to show you my idea." He opened up a small leather notebook, showing her some charts and initials in little bubbles.

He was excited about the charity. She should be happy this was the case, but her giddiness faded. "Translate this for me, o wise one." Liz motioned for him to come in the living room.

Tyler was bouncing on the balls of his feet. His excitement was contagious. "This is Happy Moments headquarters here, and this is how many people we might expect to come to a domestic project, based on the algorithm Happy Moments gave us. So, here is the potential loss of people coming because the international wow factor isn't there. Plus, it does work out to be more expensive to do a domestic project."

"This is showing us stuff we already know," Liz said slowly.

"Right. But over here, is the power we could have if

we did a slight variation on this project, and we changed the idea of it."

"You don't want it in Texas?"

"Texas is fine. But that won't be our biggest place." He looked like a kid at Christmas who just saw his presents under the tree.

"I'm all ears."

"We'll still do a project in Texas. Maybe the park, maybe something else, but the biggest part of the project will be in the community everyone lives."

"You lost me."

"Happy Moments can still put on a decent size domestic project, but we should change the marketing. Instead of going abroad, maybe we make the theme, "In your own backyard." We can have a major project in Texas, but we celebrate the weekend or the week as a day of service, regardless of whether you come into Texas to help serve."

"The point of the service project is to bond people together, get them to unite in a cause." Liz didn't like it.

"The point is to create happy moments. You don't have to travel to do that."

It was a technicality. "Yes, but the charity isn't big enough to get multiple projects going in every single city."

Tyler's smile grew wider. "We wouldn't have to set up the projects. We send out a social media marketing campaign that explains the week of service. We create a catchy hashtag, and encourage people to post their service pictures. Add a few press releases, and you create an online community of people who want to serve and be a part of something.

"The home base can still be Texas, and you can spread the word by encouraging others to come and help the charity in the future in other countries. But for this year your focus is on the city you live in. You can offer your t-shirts, or give people a color to wear so they can feel a part of the online community. People could also donate to help the park or whatever we choose, and we can work on the idea of donations for other projects, or partner with other charities."

He stopped, looking at Liz with a deep intensity. "What do you think?"

She hesitated. This wasn't the way Happy Moments did things. He didn't understand that. "You've certainly put a lot of thought into it."

His shoulders slumped. "But you don't like it." He closed his book in his lap, a deflated look on his face.

If she didn't have the history with Happy Moments, Tyler's idea would be intriguing. "I do like it. It's a great idea actually...it's just not how we've done things before."

"Sometimes it's good to change things up." There was a glimmer of hope in his voice.

"And sometimes people like the predictability and stability with doing things the way they've been done before." They'd been successful in the past.

"But you'll think about it?" He opened up his notebook, and tore the pages out, handing them to her. "The idea isn't set in stone yet."

She accepted the papers from him, feeling tingles

that reached her toes as his fingers brushed across hers. "Thanks. Yes. Let's look into this." An alarm popped on her phone. Was it *True Story*? She tagged a few e-mails to send an alarm when she received a reply.

"Something's on your mind," Tyler said. "I'm sorry. I didn't mean to drop by unexpectedly. I was excited about this idea, and didn't want to just talk all business on our date tonight."

That was thoughtful of him. Their date wouldn't be another working meal. Just the two of them. Talking about anything but the charity. Warmth spread through her, as giddy anticipation of the evening filled her. And their kiss from yesterday morning. She'd like to repeat that.

She looked around before meeting his gaze. "You're fine. I'm glad you stopped by. I'm expecting my *True Story* writing assignment this week. They didn't say exactly when it would come, but I thought it might be this weekend."

"You're really applying for their internship?" Tyler's brows rose.

"You disapprove?"

"Not at all. But...they usually choose someone with a lot of writing experience," he said it hesitantly.

"I received a Bachelor's in English and I'm finishing up my Masters in English this coming May." She didn't mean for it to come out defensive.

"Right. I remember that." He looked around the room. "I'd better leave you to your work. They are strict on their deadlines. You'll want as much time as possible to write." He paused. "You're sure you still want to go out tonight?"

"It'll be fine. I've written under deadlines before. Besides. I may not get my topic today."

Liz went to the CU game, getting there even before her family. She scanned the field. It would be a beautiful day for a game. She pulled out her phone. She'd spent the last two hours reading her old assignments, trying to guess if any of them would be good enough to show her work for *True Story*. The ideas spun around in her head. Possible topics. Possible angles. It was all impossible to guess until she received her assignment.

Liz was lost in thought until someone bumped her knees. "Hi, Cassie. Did Grip invite you to the game?"

Cassie sat down next to her, showing her the extra season ticket Liz's family owned. Cassie twisted it in her lap. "He said his family wouldn't bite." She gave a small smile. "And if I got here early I wouldn't be overwhelmed by the crowds."

Tyler had mentioned that she could be shy, but she had seemed at ease around her family at Kyle's house.

Liz nodded. "That's all true, except the biting part." She chomped her teeth with a smile.

Cassie giggled.

"No, truly, I mean it. My brothers *do* bite. You think football was crazy at my house, it was the wrestling afterward that should have won State. The boys play dirty," she said, wiggling her eyebrows. "But only with each other, so you're probably safe from teeth marks."

"It must be great to have brothers," Cassie said.

"I guess so. Don't get me wrong, I love my brothers. But I was outnumbered growing up. It would have been nice to have a sister."

"Me too." Cassie looked at the field.

"You're an only child?"

"Yes, though Tyler was kind of the big brother I never had, and I was the little sister he always wanted. It worked out." She picked at a piece of lint on her jeans.

"He told me you've always been like a sister to him."

Cassie studied Liz then nodded. "Grip wants to go for ice cream after the game. Are you coming?"

"I'm actually going to dinner with Tyler," she said, feeling her face redden.

Cassie's eyes lit up. "That's fun. What about after dinner?"

"And be the third wheel? No thanks," she said playfully.

"Tyler will come."

She bit her lip. "If he wants to, I could even the numbers."

"He'll want to. He prefers redheads."

It was half-time before Liz and Cassie chatted in detail again. During the game, Liz explained the plays to Cassie, and why Grip was brilliant at strategy. They talked casually and her parents asked Cassie a few questions, but they focused on cheering. When half-time came, her parents and Sam headed for the concessions.

"So, Tyler prefers redheads?" Liz brought the subject back to Tyler after a few minutes talking about Grip.

Cassie's giggle was infectious. Liz smiled. She would be a good match for Grip. "That's an understatement. Admittedly, he has gone on dates with women who have different hair color, but he is adamant about red hair.

"He used to watch the old movie, *Annie,* and when he was nine he said he would only love girls with curly red hair. Of course, I was distraught. There I am at four years old completely in love with Tyler, and he basically said he would never love me because of my "yellow" hair."

Liz sighed. "You poor thing. No compassion for the feelings of four-year-old girls! What did you do?"

Cassie grinned. "I cried myself to sleep after telling my mom how mean Tyler was for not loving me, and the next day I came up with the perfect plan."

Liz arched an eyebrow. "You bought a wig from the costume store?"

Cassie laughed. "I was four. I wish I had thought of that, but no. I took my markers into the bathroom, and locked the door. I was in there for probably an hour coloring my hair red with a marker. On one side the red ran out, so I used the orange, then added in purple."

"Oh no!" Liz covered her mouth with a hand.

"By the time the purple marker dried out, my mom knocked on the door to tell me it was dinner time. I hurried to the table where everyone waited for me. I proudly proclaimed that Tyler could love me because I had red hair!"

"That's an adorable story." Liz laughed. "What happened next?"

"Tyler was scolded for being insensitive and he told me that he would always love me because I was his niece. It only took twenty-seven days for all of the "washable" marker to completely wash out of my white-blond hair!"

"Wow!"

"Needless to say, I had a great collection of hats after that!" Cassie laughed.

When Liz's family came back with drinks and food, Liz veered the conversation to only topics that had nothing else to do with Tyler.

CU barely lost. Maybe bowling before a game *did* mess with Grip's head. His game was off. Bowling was a much better choice to boost Grip's mood than the typical celebration at the ice cream parlor.

"Fair warning," Liz said to Cassie, "Grip gets moody after a loss. He takes it personally. Maybe you can cheer him up or coax him into a better mood. He loves chocolate mint ice cream."

Liz said goodbye to her family, and to Cassie.

CHAPTER THIRTEEN

"Hi, Tyler," Coco said, as Tyler approached Liz's house. "I'm just leaving to film a wedding reception." She hefted a large bag of equipment over her shoulder, a tripod in her other hand. "Liz is in the living room. Here." She turned around, and opened the door for him.

"Thanks. Hope you have a great time."

"Weddings are fun. But the parties afterwards let me show off my creativity with the footage."

He went through the open door. Liz sat, chin rested on one knee pulled close to her body. Staring off into space. He had to give it to her. That was an expression he knew well. One of being lost inside a story and a character's head. When she didn't look toward him, he grinned. She was completely lost in thought. He closed the door, but she still didn't move. He knocked lightly on the door from the inside. "Hi. Coco let me in."

She jerked to a standing position. "Oh. Hi. Sorry. I

was thinking about your Happy Moments proposal. I really like it." She picked up her purse from the couch. "Shall we?"

He nodded. "You look beautiful."

A small smile flitted across her perfect lips. "And you're handsome."

He opened the car door for her. Nerves filled him. He'd been helping Liz for a week now. Just because this was an official date, didn't mean it had to be weird.

They pulled into La Pergola, his favorite Italian restaurant in Colorado. The upscale place had a distinct New York feel to it.

It didn't take long to get their order in. He got his usual, shrimp scampi, and Liz looked surprised as he ordered his food with an Italian accent. He'd picked up a few words from his Italian neighbors in New York.

A few minutes later, the waiter brought bread and small shallow bowls. He poured a few different kinds of olive oil into the dishes, and added balsamic vinegar.

She tore a corner of the loaf, and swirled it generously in the oil. "You mentioned earlier that *True Story* picks people with more experience. Tell me about that. I still haven't received an e-mail back from them yet. I was sure it would come this week."

"I haven't done work for them in years. But they are the top in the industry. They select writers from the most prestigious newspapers and magazines. It surprises me that you want to work there, because you're working for a law firm instead of in journalism."

Liz blew out a breath. "It's been difficult to find a

writing job, and expect them to be flexible to my family circumstances. Most require working on the weekends."

"And you're the cheerleader, helping everyone else on the weekends." He admired her for being the cheerleader, but she only seemed to see her value in helping others, not in helping herself.

She sighed. "I like being the cheerleader."

"But you've put all of your dreams on hold for them." She was smart and capable, and yet, she seemed to put her whole life on pause the moment any member of her family needed something.

"Not *all* of my dreams." She straightened her silverware, not looking up.

He'd hit a nerve. It wasn't great timing to be on a date and talk about this obviously sensitive topic, but he had to know why she put herself last. "But you don't take the opportunities that could help you achieve your dreams."

"You don't think I have a chance with *True Story*." Her shoulders slumped, her eyes staring at the table.

He reached across the table, covering her hand with his. "Liz, you have a chance. They'll give you an opportunity to impress them. Your passion and love for writing will help your voice shine through your work." He squeezed her hand. "You can do this." She had a determination to achieve whatever she put her mind to—like the rest of her family.

Her posture relaxed. "Thank you. I—"

The server interrupted Liz with their food, placing the dishes in front of them.

Liz moved her hand from under Tyler's, taking a sip of water, and he immediately felt the loss of her touch.

The shrimp was arranged in a spiral on a bed of pasta, filling the entire rectangle plate, perfectly unaware that its arrival had just killed a moment.

The server offered freshly grated Parmesan cheese, and Liz accepted. She took a bite of her noodles and sighed.

"This is delicious. How is your food?" he asked.

"I'm going to eat this whole thing and not say a word, I like it that much."

They talked more about *True Story* and laughed over funny stories he told about New York and crazy stories she told about Happy Moments. As Tyler walked Liz out to his car, it felt too soon to end the night.

He drove in the direction of her house. "Dinner was fun. Thanks for coming with me."

"It was delicious food, and even better company," she said. "Oh. I forgot to mention it earlier, but Cassie invited us to join her and Grip tonight after dinner."

"They're on a date?" Grip didn't seem like Cassie's type.

She laughed. "You haven't noticed that they like each other? It seemed obvious during our bowling game."

"I guess I've been busy. I hadn't really noticed." Mostly, he'd been paying attention to Liz, and nobody else. She filled his every waking thought.

Maybe that was why her putting her dreams on hold for her family bothered him so much. He was falling hard for her. He wanted her to be happy. To achieve the dreams that she worked so hard for, not put them on the back burner because she lived her life cheering for others. It seemed unfair.

"So." Liz cleared her throat. "Did you want to join them? I mean, it's up to you, but it sounds like fun."

"Let them know we're on our way."

Liz pulled out her phone and squealed.

"Is everything okay?"

"That was definitely a happy squeal! I just got my e-mail from *True Story.*"

He hoped it was good news. "What does it say?"

"It's your typical form letter, and then this little gem: *'Please write an article on a current topic of your choice. Your choice should reflect your passion for your particular subject. Please do not duplicate a topic already in your submitted writings. You have twenty-four hours from the sending of this e-mail to reply with your finished article attached.'*"

"Wow. That's great news." He was proud of her. "What will you pick for your topic?"

"If I can't use anything I've previously written about, that eliminates all of the best topics and material I've ever used. So, Happy Moments is out. It's sad, but aside from school, and cheering at football games, Happy Moments *is* what I do. It's about all I do."

"I'm sure it'll be great no matter what subject you decide on," he said.

"I'm one step closer to securing the internship."

He wished the date would last longer, but Liz should go work on her article. She didn't have very much time, and every minute they were together was less time that she'd be able to concentrate on it. He didn't want to be another obstacle in her way. She already let her family have a lot of say in her life. He pulled up in front of her house, and parked the car, and opened the door for her. "Good luck working on your article tonight."

She took his arm. "Trying to get rid of me already?" She laughed. "I guess we've spent so much time together lately, you're probably sick of me by now."

"Not what I meant at all. I just don't want to keep you from reaching your dreams." He had to stay firm on this. She had twenty-four hours to finish her assignment, on top of everything else she had going on. "How about a rain check with Cassie and Grip?"

"Okay. A rain check works."

He gave her a quick kiss at her door, wishing the evening with her wasn't over so soon. But he knew it would be for the best. As much as he wanted to spend more time with her, he didn't want to be the reason she didn't focus on *True Story*.

"You're home late." Cassie smiled up from her book. A lamp illuminated the chair with the only light in the room.

He locked the door behind him. After dropping off Liz, he drove aimlessly around. The look in Liz's eyes after he gave her a swift kiss on the doorstep was not how he wanted to remember the evening. He couldn't shake it off. "Waiting up for me?"

"Well, Mom and Dad won't be back until tomorrow, so someone has to."

He ruffled her hair as he passed by her chair. "I haven't felt so much concern after a date since I was a senior in high school."

"The benefits of living out of state."

"Or the non-benefits." Tyler sat in the chair across from her. "So, are you going to interrogate me, or should I go get my own book?"

Cassie raised an eyebrow. "You want me to question you? I'll take it. So, you like her?"

Tyler nodded. "What's not to like? She's smart, pretty, loyal to her family." And she was fun. The whipped cream fight and kiss ran through his head making him smile. He'd wished their doorstep kiss held that kind of emotion, but it hadn't.

"I've noticed that. All that flirting during bowling. She asked about you during the football game."

"Did she? What about?"

"Oh, lots of random stuff. She wanted to know about your writing, and what you were like growing up. I told her about the time I colored my hair with markers. She had a good laugh over that one. She seems to like you a lot."

If the kissing yesterday were any indication, he'd come up with that conclusion already. The feel of her in his arms felt perfect. She fit.

Tyler grabbed a book off the table. He thumbed

through it, but he couldn't pretend to be interested in Jim's grammar book. He cleared his throat. "Did she say she likes me?"

Cassie shrugged. "It seems obvious to me."

He let Cassie's statement sink in. He had two more weeks in Colorado. Hopefully that was enough time to finish his last few interviews and help Liz with planning the service project. Two weeks didn't seem long enough. But he'd need to shadow Kyle for a month before the writer's conference in New York started.

"I like her by the way. She has my approval." Cassie kept her face behind her book.

It was time for a topic change. "What about you and Grip?"

"He's very nice. And funny and sweet." She put her book down. The blush on her cheeks deepened. "You know, I think I'd better get some sleep. Goodnight. Thanks for the chat."

Tyler sat in the front room a little longer, wishing he was still with Liz.

CHAPTER FOURTEEN

Two hours after Tyler dropped Liz off, she still stared at her computer screen, typing only a few words at a time. A giddy anticipation had filled her insides when she first read the e-mail containing her article assignment. An article on a subject of her choice should be easy, but the mostly blank page on the screen didn't inspire any words.

This *True Story* assignment was proving harder for her than she cared to admit. She was supposed to write about something she was passionate about, but without repeating any of the same topics she'd already used. It was a challenge.

She struggled to get fifty words on the page.

She grabbed the stack of papers Tyler left her with for his idea for Happy Moments. He had done research and found a park not too far from Happy Moments head-quarters in Dallas that had tried to raise donations for improvements, but had failed to reach their goal. They put the project on hold indefinitely, due to the lack of support. Liz looked through the proposal.

They were asking for extra trees, a pathway around the park, a new playground area, and a few pavilions with picnic areas. He wasn't suggesting they build the concrete path, but there was a lot that could be done to fix up the run-down park.

They could help with building the pavilions, and installing park benches. Planting trees was doable, as was other ornamental bushes and flowers. Maybe they could add a splash pad or a climbing wall. They could design a bigger playground area, and maybe make it themed, so kids could have different forts to play in, instead of just a typical slide and set.

The more she went through this, the more excited she became. Tyler had come up with a wonderful idea. There was enough work to keep volunteers busy for a week. This could really work. It wasn't the way they normally ran things, but it looked like the best solution they could come up with in their limited time. Though it was nice to gather a big group together for service, organizing a service day could provide additional happy moments. The idea made her heart swell.

She stifled a yawn, about to turn in for the night, when an idea hit her. She knew what she was going to write on for *True Story*. She pulled up a new document and her fingers flew furiously over the keys, trying to capture all of the stray thoughts. She wouldn't write about Happy Moments, but she could write about her passion for helping others, and the importance of making a difference in others' lives. Everyone needs a cheerleader.

Liz woke with a start to her phone alarm buzzing. She'd fallen asleep in the middle of typing. The letter E filled twenty-eight electronic pages. She skimmed through her document to see if anything she'd written last night made sense. She had a few coherent thoughts, and she still had twelve hours to write her article and turn it in. That was plenty of time.

"You're up early," Jenny said, coming into the living room.

"Or up late still," Liz said, fingering her curls.

"Work?" Jenny gestured to Liz's laptop.

"Tyler came up with a brilliant idea for Happy Moments, so when I was stuck last night on my *True Story* article, I went through the details."

"Sounds like fun. I want to hear all about it over breakfast."

Liz joined Jenny at the kitchen table and filled her in about Tyler and his idea. The more she told Jenny about it, the more excited she was for the project. It was a viable solution. She pulled up her e-mail to write to Kyle's assistant to confirm the details of the park and get a contact number for the one who arranged the fundraiser for the park project this past summer. As she clicked send, Liz noticed the *True Story* e-mail, and pulled it up, going over the details before she wrote the article.

She was about to close her e-mail, when the time and date stamp at the top of the e-mail caught her eye. It had been sent at 8:30 a.m. yesterday morning. Liz froze. There had to be some mistake. She hadn't received the e-mail until after her dinner with Tyler. She'd checked every hour for the last week, to make sure she didn't miss the e-mail. What happened?

Kyle's assistant called, probably wanting more details on the summer project. She was tempted to answer it, but pushed ignore. Panic mode was no time for phone calls.

8:05 a.m. Liz clicked into her e-mail on her phone. Sure enough the time on the e-mail there was 8:30 p.m. Then she refreshed her phone, and the time stamp updated. Her stomach felt full of lead.

Had she known the deadline was earlier in the day, she would have written instead of going out to dinner. But she didn't know. *True Story* wouldn't take her excuse. And twenty minutes wouldn't give her time to talk through her article with Tyler, or to have him proofread it.

She pulled up the notes she'd made, and her fingers flew across the keyboard. Her brain didn't keep up with them as she wrote line after line of text. She skimmed through it. It wasn't her best work. Not even close. But she had to turn something in. She continued to write.

Waves of stress swam around her, but she couldn't tackle that now. She needed to complete the article. That was the only thing she could do. Wishing she had already told Kyle she couldn't fix his Happy Moments problem was useless right now.

She wanted Tyler's feedback, but the article needed to be submitted in less than five minutes. And thinking of Tyler automatically spun her brain up on kissing him, and another minute sped by as she hit reply to the *True Story* e-mail and attached the document.

She pressed send after only spending twenty minutes on the draft. She resisted the urge to proofread the document now. She'd sent it with two minutes to spare, and if she found a mistake now, it would only make her feel anxious that she couldn't fix it. She stared at the screen an extra second, holding her breath, but there was no instantaneous reply.

Later that day Liz connected with Kyle's assistant on the phone. Once she hung up she called Tyler to tell him the good news. She wanted to go with Tyler's idea.

"You really like the idea about the park?" Tyler asked.

It hadn't been her first choice, but the idea grew on her, and now it wasn't just a backup plan. "I think it's exactly what we should do. I was able to get the phone number of the guy in charge of raising money for this project, thanks to Kyle's assistant, and he is willing to help partner on it."

"Mr. Johnson will be a great resource. He had several bids out to get the supplies at cost, and several companies were willing to donate a few of their employees to oversee the building of the pavilions and the park."

"Thank you! This will be great! Kyle will love this." And she loved collaborating with him on this project, and couldn't wait to see him again. Butterflies fluttered all through her.

~

Over the next week they worked tirelessly. Liz even took off work to finish it. They looked over the final proposal for the service project. Kyle was going to love it, and it felt rewarding being able to complete this project.

Tyler gave her a hug. "This calls for celebration."

"What did you have in mind?" She sent Kyle an e-mail about the project. He had given his approval of the project, but wanted more specific details and marketing ideas before they finished their work.

"How about New York?"

What did he mean by that? "You're going to buy me a state?"

"There's always a good spot to celebrate there."

"I'll be there next summer." She was in the middle of classes. She couldn't just leave.

"What about coming to New York with me for a writer's conference in a month?"

"The Digital Quill Conference?" Her voice cracked with excitement. It was an exclusive conference, but getting invited advanced careers quickly.

"That's the one. Huge convention. Lots of classes. I'm one of the keynotes," he said. "It could be a lot of fun."

Spending a week with Tyler, in New York. It sounded perfect. But was it only because she was interested in writing? Or was there another reason why he asked her? Over the last week that they'd worked on the final details for the summer project, she'd looked forward to each day more than the last. He was inside her thoughts constantly. But was that crazy? Should she be cautious? Maybe she was reading too much into his invitation. Just because he filled all of her brain's waking hours with him, didn't mean he felt the same way. "It does sound fun. I'll look into it."

"It's sold out, but I have access to a few extra tickets. I can set you up with a VIP package, maybe introduce you to *True Story* while we're there."

True Story might take weeks to get back to her. She wasn't holding her breath every time she opened her e-mail like she had the first three days after submitting her article. It would come soon. Or maybe if she went to the conference she'd make an impression on them, and they'd send her response quicker. But Tyler wanted her to come. Yes, *True Story* would be there, but Tyler would be there too. "I'd love to meet *True Story*, but I don't want to use your connections to meet them."

"Networking isn't using others."

She paused. She could meet them without Tyler introducing her. She could do it herself. She didn't like the idea of using others' connections to get what she wanted. That's what Rick had done. "Let me think about it. I want to, but that's a full week to figure out work and school."

"I'll be in town for another week, but I can always e-mail you the info when I'm in Texas or back in New York if you decide you want to come," he said.

Was their time together drawing to a close so quickly? Between *True Story* and Happy Moments, she hadn't thought about it. "I didn't realize you'd be leaving so soon."

"We've finished up the charity planning on time, so I'll keep my original plane ticket to Dallas. Kyle wanted a few weeks under his belt playing this season before I shadowed him. Then I head back to New York to get ready for the conference."

Liz put on a smile, even as her heart sank into her stomach. He was leaving. Of course he was. He wasn't a permanent fixture in Colorado. In her head she knew that, but it still came as a shock to hear him say it. Things were going so well between them. She chewed on her lip, wondering if she should consider a long-distance relation-ship with him. She had a week to figure out how to bring it up without seeming too forward.

CHAPTER FIFTEEN

L iz hardly saw Tyler during his last week in town. He had crammed in more interviews and second interviews with family, friends, and a few of the other high school teachers Kyle had. He was booked morning and night, and Liz didn't realize how much time they'd spent together working on the charity and flirting, until he was almost non-existent.

He had sent her a few texts between his interviews, and she replied as quick as she could, hoping to hold onto a small conversation. Then he'd be in another interview. She didn't want to have to get used to him not being around. The idea stung a little.

She had buried herself in work and school for the week, grateful for a chance to catch up in a class that she'd pushed off in favor of getting Happy Moments planned. She seemed to work twice as fast, though she spent a decent amount of time thinking about Tyler. He was never far from her thoughts.

Tyler would be picking her up any moment. Two days ago, he texted her that he had a question for her. He wanted to discuss it over dinner. The thought left an excited shiver down her spine. He was going to ask about pursuing a long-distance relationship. They could make it work. She had taken extra care on her outfit and loaded her hair with product to keep the curliness in check.

She answered when he rang the doorbell. Buzzing excitement exploded through her as he gave her a quick kiss, and entwined his fingers with hers. "You're beautiful."

She breathed in his cologne. *I've missed you.* "You're looking rather dashing yourself." *Dashing? Really, Liz?* Ugh. There were a hundred words to choose from and she felt herself tongue tied.

He led her to his car, and opened her door.

"How were your interviews this week?" She hated that she asked, when really what she wanted to know was if he missed her now that they weren't spending time everyday together.

"Interviews were long. I had to cram them in almost back to back to make sure I could get as much information as I needed." He glanced over at her, and continued to drive toward the freeway. "It wasn't nearly as fun as working on the charity plans together."

Liz smiled. He was earning points.

They chatted and laughed on the way to Denver. It all seemed very trivial. She wanted deep, meaningful conversation. But maybe he was saving that for the restaurant. *That's it. Good filler until we eat dinner.*

"This is one of my favorite places." Liz's fingers found Tyler's again as they entered the upscale Mexican restaurant, Fiesta Grill. The feel of his hands on hers made everything feel right.

"It's good." He leaned in close, tickling her ear with his breath. "But there's a really good restaurant in New York I'd love to take you to."

She smiled at him, but was cut off from responding as the maître d' looked at Tyler and then immediately ushered a hostess to their side. "Welcome Mr. Lake," the balding man said. "Always a pleasure to have you back."

Tyler responded politely to the greeting and whispered to Liz. "I held a dinner here for one of my first book launches. It's crazy how people still remember that."

Liz nodded. People did the same thing for her family. Anywhere Kyle had looked at or went into once, seemed to claim a part of his fame. That was compounded by having her oldest brother Ron, and her dad also in the NFL stardom.

They were seated, and the waiter came to explain the specials. They looked over their menus, and Tyler ordered the tableside guacamole with their drinks.

"Speaking of New York, have you given more thought to the Digital Quill Conference?"

Liz smiled. The warm-up question. The prequel to him asking about the logistics of a long-term relationship. She took a sip of water. "I have. I've cleared it with work. And all of my professors seem very supportive of going to it. Two of them mentioned that tickets are hard to come by. You left out the fact that I'd be the envy of the faculty for going."

"I told you I have a VIP ticket I can give away."

"I'm excited. I looked through the link you sent me. It seems like a great place to learn."

"And network."

Network? The fancy word for using other people's connections to get what they wanted. She waved her hand in the air. "Or just learn. And I hear there is at least one talented keynote speaker."

"Yes. Ryan Jefferson always draws a big crowd."

She swatted playfully at his hand. "I meant *you*."

The waiter brought the guacamole, mixed it to their preferences, and presented it to the table. After making their order, Liz loaded up a chip, and took a bite. The flavors exploded in her mouth.

"This is delicious." Liz took another chip, dipping it in the fresh salsa. "I might not have room for my entrée with an appetizer like that."

"You can take it home for leftovers," he said.

"Good point."

By the time their entrees came out, they had polished off the entire appetizer.

Liz tried her steak fajitas and they commented on the food. Finally, she couldn't stand the suspense. She cleared her throat, then drank more water. "You had a question for me?" Their eyes locked. She'd miss those eyes over the next month. Maybe they could Facetime every night.

Tyler smiled. "I knew if I told you, you'd remember to bring it up. Okay, here it goes. I've been gathering all of my research for Kyle's biography. I think I have all of the different angles except one. I'm missing Kyle's story on how he and Kandice got together. Your mom dropped a few hints here and there. Kyle mentioned you were instrumental. Even Grip said something about it, but no details.

"I ask follow-up questions, but all of them have said the same thing. Talk to you about it. You mentioned it would take a whole dinner to get through the story, without a work deadline. So, I thought I'd ask if you'd tell me the abbreviated version of the story."

Liz's jaw dropped. She quickly gathered a bite on her fork and shoved it in her mouth, forcing her jaw to move upward. *That was the question he wanted to ask?* Heat flooded her cheeks. He didn't want to define their relationship. He wanted details for his story. She swallowed her half-chewed food hard. They'd had fun getting to know each other the last few weeks. But it was based around getting their jobs done.

He was writing Kyle's biography and needed information. She was forced into taking his help on the charity. No. Not quite. She wasn't forced to take his help. He'd offered, and thanks to the tight deadline, it had made the most sense at the time.

She felt stupid. They'd gone out together to eat. They'd been on a few dates. But most of it seemed to revolve around their jobs. They both had a job to do.

Happy Moments was essentially planned. Only a few more things to follow up on, and it was all a list she would handle herself. His time in Colorado was coming to an end, and he wanted the rest of the story. It made sense, but the loss of anticipation of the question she hoped he would ask stung.

"Liz?" Tyler's concerned look came into focus. "You don't have to tell me any details you don't want to. Biographies can't cover every single detail of a person's life. Not even all of the highlights will make it into the final draft."

She nodded mechanically. Like she'd woken up with a pinched nerve in her neck. "I can tell you the story. I planned to tell you anyway. It's not a big deal."

"Are you okay if I record it?"

She forced a smile, then she shook the feeling aside. She didn't want to ruin the last few hours with Tyler by being in a bad mood over her dashed expectations. Kyle's biography didn't deserve a tainted view. "Sure. I wrote a paper on the story during my undergrad. I changed the names so it wasn't obvious I was talking about Kyle and Kandice, and I changed the football references to baseball, but you get the basic idea of the story. I'm happy to send that to you too, if it's helpful."

"I'd love to read it." He put his cell phone on the table. The recording app counted up and the red button on the bottom blinked.

"How did Kyle and Kandice's love story start?" Tyler asked.

"We were shopping in her family's bookstore. As a

fifteen-year-old, the first time I saw them together, I didn't initially pick up on the tension. I only saw the sparks flying around the bookstore." The waves across the screen moved in patterns as she spoke.

"What was your specific involvement with getting Kyle and Kandice together?"

Liz smiled, holding back the mischievous feeling she had whenever she thought about how much she helped Kyle and Kandice. "I asked Kandice for her number, since Kyle wouldn't. At the time, it meant I earned riding shot-gun over Grip in the car. It was obvious to me they were both interested in each other."

"Kyle doesn't seem like the shy type to me."

"He's not. I found out later they'd dated in high school, but it ended badly. Kandice gave him a black eye, and they didn't speak for the rest of high school. Of course, I didn't know all of that when I asked for her number, for Kyle."

She took another bite of her food, and then continued. "I followed up with Kyle, and finally he told me he called her, and they were going out. After the date, I asked how it went, and he was way too vague for someone who was clearly interested in her.

"I ended up running into Kandice a few days later when she dropped off a niece and nephew at the summer day camps at the high school. She was nice to me, but made it clear that she wasn't going to go out with Kyle again."

"So how did they get together?" He leaned forward in his chair.

"I broke my femur during the cheerleading day camp."

"Ouch." He winced.

"It was painful on so many levels. But that's a different story. Kandice was in the stands, watching her niece in my day camp. My parents were on an anniversary trip, so Kyle was filling in for my dad's football camp for the week." Every detail was still so clear, though it was eight years ago. She could almost smell the freshly cut grass on the field, mixed with fabric softener she'd used on her cheerleading uniform, and the smell of her blood on both.

She blinked, focusing on the part of that day that was crucial to the love story. "Kyle was on the field next to me. Kandice had come down to the field, and Kyle wanted to ride in the ambulance, so he handed her the keys and asked her to meet us at the hospital so he had a ride home. She agreed."

"What happened next?"

"I went into surgery and was groggy for hours. When I came out, Kyle and Kandice were both still there. I talked to each of them separately because the doctor was strict about visitors. It's amazing what people will tell you when they think you're on your deathbed. Not that I needed to play up the dramatics."

Tyler cocked his head. "You manipulated them?"

"More it was encouraging them. Maybe I manipulated the situation. I mean I didn't break my femur and end my high school cheerleading career just to push them together, but I played it up. They both confided in me about their past breakup in high school, and I could see the misunderstanding for what it was.

"So, I maybe apologized for the other without letting each of them know what I was doing. And I made both of them promise me that they would go out with the other at least three times before they gave up on the possibility of a relationship. And I made them promise not to say anything to each other about the deal."

"And that worked?"

"I pushed and nudged very carefully. They figured out that they were in love." She wouldn't have Kandice as a sister-in-law if she hadn't helped them along. And without Kandice, Kyle never would have started Happy Moments. It was worth the stress she put into their relationship. "They didn't realize until after they were engaged that I had anything to do with it."

"You're a subtle matchmaker then?"

Her grin widened. "It's an art really. It takes years of experience to get this proficient, and I was only fifteen at the time."

"Humble much?"

"Nope. Not when I'm the sole reason they're together." She leaned closer to the mic. "So yes. I want the credit for it in his biography. I did the tough work."

"Ha. Deal."

"I knew they'd be right for each other, even if they were too stubborn to see it for themselves."

Tyler clicked off the recording app. "Wow. That's a great story."

"I'm a good matchmaker."

"But you're an even better storyteller," he said.

She felt her cheeks warm at his praise. "Thank you."

"No. Thank you for sharing. Now I see why Kyle wanted me to get the story straight from you. It's perfect." He leaned back. "Dessert?"

Liz shook her head. "I don't think I can eat any more. As it is, I'm taking half of it home in a box."

On the way home Tyler held her hand, stroking her fingers. But the gesture felt like a goodbye. The anticipation of a long-distance relationship deflated during the meal. She shouldn't have jumped to conclusions. They'd only gone on a few dates. So what if they'd spent a few weeks working on a major project together? That didn't mean anything besides him being a nice, helpful guy. Except for those kisses. The emotion swelled inside her.

"I'm flying from Dallas to New York the Friday before the conference starts. Originally I was going to work on my speech that weekend..." He paused. "But, maybe I'll have time at Kyle's house, in between shadowing him to finish my speech early."

"Sounds like a plan." She caught the underlying reason he would tell her. She shouldn't expect him to call or text too often because he'd be extra busy.

"Would you want to come out a few days before the conference and do some sightseeing? There's not a lot of time during the conference days to really experience it."

Hope bubbled inside of her. "You'd give me a tour of the city?"

"There's a lot to see and do there. It might give you an

idea if you really want to make the move from Colorado to New York."

"That's only if I secure the job at *True Story*."

"Think about it. It would be fun."

She didn't need to think about it. "I'd love to."

CHAPTER SIXTEEN

Tyler arrived in Dallas two days after he last spoke with Liz. After a restful evening, he set up early Tuesday morning in Kyle's library. The small laptop fan whirred, breaking the silence that surrounded him.

Liz agreed to come to New York early, so he didn't have any spare time. His upcoming speech for the Digital Quill Conference loomed over him, and he needed to make headway on the biography. Writing at Kyle's house in between shadowing him would give him the best chance to focus on the biography before he'd be back to work on his next epic fantasy.

The blank document on his laptop remained an empty canvas. Several times he added sentences. But each time he deleted them again, one character at a time. His upcoming speech was going to be short if he couldn't think through his fingers.

He picked up his phone. It was too early to call Liz.

He'd wait a few more hours. Maybe he could catch her at breakfast. The thought of breakfast with her brought back a rush of memories and their first kiss.

Two hours of typing and deleting later, he had a few pages brainstorming his ideas for his speech. It wasn't long, but it was original.

He picked up his phone, and called Liz.

A mumbled voice answered the phone. "Hello?"

"Good morning."

Liz yawned on the other end. "If you say so. I was counting on at least another four minutes of sleep."

Tyler laughed.

"Does Kyle want to talk about Happy Moments right now?" Her voice suddenly sounded panicked. "I don't think I can run through all of it before my class starts."

He swallowed hard. "Oh, no. He hasn't mentioned that to me. I think our plan was still for this evening."

"Oh. Okay. I guess I just assumed that was why you were calling." She paused. "Why did you call?"

Tyler drummed his fingers across the dark wood desk. "I missed you." He sounded like a teenager. A completely sappy teenager.

Was her startled sound a good sign or a bad one? "I've missed you too. Finishing up the last of the charity paper-work isn't the same without you." She giggled.

"So... I will talk to you tonight then?"

"I'm still planning on it."

"Great—" The double French doors to the library swung into the room.

Kandice came in. "Oh. Hi, Tyler. I thought Kyle was

in here. He's probably still working out downstairs. Anyway, breakfast is ready when you'd like it." She paused. "Oh, sorry. I didn't realize you were on the phone."

"It's okay," Tyler said. "I have to go," he told Liz. "Kandice is serving breakfast."

"You're in for a treat. She makes amazing breakfast food."

"It smells good from here."

"Bye."

"See ya."

"Was that Cassie? She is adorable. You're welcome to bring her along any time you'd like."

"It was Liz actually."

"Oh. Right, last-minute prep for your meeting tonight."

She left the room before he could correct her, and he followed her into the kitchen. "I'm going to be a fly on the wall during the day. I'll be observing life, but I'm trying to let you have your own schedules, without you worrying about attending to a houseguest."

"I'll do my best, but I love entertaining. Omelet bar for breakfast today." She handed him a bowl. "Choose your toppings, and how many eggs you want, and I'll do the rest." She smiled brightly at him.

"Thanks."

Kyle came up to the kitchen, a towel around his neck. "Hi, hon. I'm going to shower, and I'll be out in ten. Good morning, Tyler."

"Hey."

Tyler filled his bowl with mushrooms, tomatoes, peppers, green onions, ham, spinach, cheese, and basil. He handed Kandice the bowl. "Three eggs would be great."

"Coming right up. You're not allergic to any spices are you?"

"No. I can handle heat."

"Great," she said, shaking several different ingredients into the egg mixture. She poured it onto the frying pan, and filled two more bowls with vegetables. Kyle's bowl was three times the size of Tyler's. "I make him two omelets to start."

They chatted for a few minutes, and Kandice pulled the frying pan off the flame, and slid a perfect omelet onto a plate. She garnished it with a few tomatoes, and a basil leaf.

"This looks delicious. Thank you."

She shrugged. "Omelets are winners that way. So. Tell me before Kyle comes in. That phone call to Liz wasn't really about the charity meeting tonight, was it?"

Tyler's fork stilled in the middle of the omelet. He swallowed. "We've spent a lot of time together over the last month, working on the charity."

"She's a lot of fun," Kandice said.

Among others things. "She's thoughtful and such a good writer." He had loved reading her college paper of Kyle and Kandice's love story on the plane. She had a captivating writing style. He thought of the upcoming conference together and wished it was sooner. He missed her already.

Kandice smiled. "She *is* thoughtful. She's the reason I gave Kyle a chance. I turned him down before she talked some sense into me."

"She told me her version. But you could always add more to it." Tyler hoped she would tell him more about Liz.

"I'm sure Liz's version is accurate. I sometimes wonder if she planned the whole thing from the beginning."

"Hard to plan getting your femur broken."

"That's true. But without it, I doubt I would have listened to her about Kyle. That girl." She shook her head.

Tyler savored each bite. The omelet popped with a slight peppery garlic taste.

Kandice went back to cooking the omelets, pulling them off the stove, and garnishing both of them with tomatoes and basil like she had with Tyler's.

Kyle walked into the room, and gave his wife a kiss. "What are we talking about?" he asked.

She handed Kyle his omelets. "Just reliving how we got together with Tyler. Liz told him the *whole* story."

Kyle nodded. "Good thing you heard it from her. You'd never believe the manipulation without her side." He laughed. "Not that I mind. She went to a lot of trouble to get us together."

Kandice swatted his arm. "She didn't manipulate. She suggested."

"She practically made you go out with me, while pretending she was on her deathbed."

"It worked, didn't it?"

"It was perfect. I love you." He kissed her before she could respond.

Tyler focused on the omelet in front of him, missing Liz more at that moment. He hadn't realized when he agreed to write Kyle's biography, that delving into someone else's life would highlight the vacancy in his own. His writing career was a successful part of him, but it was also an isolating part. He wanted more. Someone to share his life with.

Writing epic fantasy novels never left him feeling empty, before. *Before what?* Before he tried a new genre? It wasn't just the biography—It was Liz. He pushed a bite of tomato and egg around on his plate, before putting it in his mouth and chewing. The breakfast he and Liz had shared together popped into his mind. Maybe kissing over eggs would be just as exciting as kissing during a whipped cream fight.

Tyler shadowed Kyle all day. Tuesday was Kyle's day off. He rotated through his home gym a few times, ate four meals, and took a few phone calls. He coordinated with his charity.

"You keep your cool all the time?" Tyler asked when Kyle finished a heated phone call.

"My dad always taught me it was the easiest way to do it. Store up the energy and adrenaline. Tackle your problems on the field. Don't let them rattle your real life."

"Wise words."

"I owe my success to him. He helped me see the maturity I needed to play football with passion, if I really wanted to make it a career. He once told me that everyone I play against is going to be better than me in some way. I can't get cocky about my skills or I'll be weak against my opponent. I know he was talking about football. But more often than not all of his advice was about the game of life."

Tyler scribbled Kyle's words down. He knew from shadowing Kyle's dad that Jack was always teaching his players about life first, football second. It was a smart way to look at sports. "You have a very supportive family."

"Everyone needs a cheerleader. That's another phrase from my dad."

"Even the ones not playing," Tyler said. Liz needed a cheerleader.

Liz called. "Hi, guys. I'm driving home from work. How is the reception?"

"You're on speaker and we can hear you," Kyle said. Tyler felt Kyle's gaze on him, but kept his own face neutral, looking at the phone on the desk.

"Tyler, while I drive, maybe you can fill Kyle in on our plans, and then I'll chime in when I'm at my computer."

"You're sure you don't want to present it?"

"I don't mind."

"Okay. Feel free to interrupt and add in any details you want to." Tyler pulled out a folder with several pages in it and handed it to Kyle. "This is the final proposal."

Kyle opened up the packet, and read. He flipped through the pages, then went back through them again. "This is very thorough."

"I know that a service project that has a small base isn't how we normally do it," Liz said, "but our hope is that those interested who can't travel to Dallas for the week, can participate wherever they are.

"We've created a hashtag so people can post their own experiences online and join in the conversation. We even thought about having shirts available for others outside of Dallas, and then we'll have a list of what everyone worked on, online. They can fill out the volunteer form, and still be part of a service experience, even if it's not at the main project."

"I can see why you wanted to show me this in person," Kyle said. "It's a lot to go through without some guidance."

"We also put a list together of service projects that could be organized by smaller groups locally." Tyler pulled out a page from his own folder to show Kyle, who poured over the details.

"Hold on. I'm getting out of my car," Liz said. They heard the door shut and her steps echoing on the sidewalk. "Okay. I'm inside. What do you think of the plan, Kyle?"

Kyle smiled. "This sounds like a promising idea. You've thought through a lot."

"I think it will be easy to present at the charity ball. I wrote a draft for you, if you want to make the announcement."

"This is your idea, Liz. I'm not taking credit for it."

"If we want to be technical, this is Tyler's idea. I just put it in the Happy Moments format and generated the paperwork."

"It was a joint collaboration," Tyler chimed in. He glanced at Kyle.

Kyle raised his eyebrows. A small smile appeared, and he leaned toward the phone, clasping his hands on the table. "It's settled. You can both present it."

"Or I can let Tyler take the whole thing. It'd be great for his publicity of your biography that he's also involved in the charity."

Kyle gave Tyler a questioning look. "What do you want to do?"

"I'm fine either way."

"Kyle, let Tyler finish the speech and present it." Liz's voice came across the phone. "I'm swamped with school projects. I need to get a writing portfolio together before I leave for the conference, and that won't give me much time with finals looming right after Thanksgiving. Besides Tyler is already in speech writing mode with the Digital Quill Conference."

Tyler nodded. "I'll do it, Liz. Focus on your portfolio for the next two weeks. You'll want to feel prepared to sit down with *True Story*."

"I didn't know you were going to a writer's conference," Kyle said.

"I'm tagging along with Tyler. He's going to show me the ropes in New York, and help me get my feet wet."

"Well, maybe you can introduce Tyler at the charity ball?" Kyle asked.

"Sure. I can do that," Liz said through the speaker.

Normally presenting gave him a rolling feeling in his stomach, but the idea of Liz next to him on stage felt more like an adrenaline rush.

"We've got our plan," Kyle said. "Thanks for all of your work on this Liz. I know it was a sacrifice for both of you."

"Happy to be your cheerleader. Tell Kandice hi for me. Talk to you later, Tyler?"

Tyler glanced at Kyle before responding. "Yes. I'll call you tonight."

"Okay, bye."

Kyle leaned back in his chair away from the desk after they ended the call. "You're calling her later?"

Tyler swallowed. "We're going over our plans for New York."

Kyle put a hand on Tyler's shoulder. "Don't break her heart."

"I'm not planning to."

Kyle let out a bark of a laugh. "I doubt many people plan to."

CHAPTER SEVENTEEN

Liz scanned the horizon before the plane touched down at JFK airport. The buildings sparkled in the sunlight. Her knee bounced against the seat. The woman next to her glared.

"Sorry. I've never been to New York City."

The woman nodded, but turned away.

She looked around as she disembarked from the jetway, spotting Tyler wearing a sweater and leather jacket. He leaned against a wall adjacent to a restaurant, his eyes focused in her direction.

The last few weeks with only the texting and calls seemed too long.

"Welcome to New York." He gave her a hug, and took her carry-on luggage. "It's a good thing we came into the same terminal, or I would have had to meet you in the other part of the airport."

"I can't believe I'm finally here." It was a dream come

true. She threaded her hand in his as they exited the terminal.

They took the Airtrain. Liz kept her eyes focused on everything passing outside, squeezing Tyler's hand each time something grabbed her attention. Soon they transferred to the subway to take them the rest of the way into the city.

"We'll check in at the hotel, drop our bags off, and then, it's time to sightsee," Tyler said.

Once inside her room, Liz changed out of the clothes she'd traveled in. A dinging on her phone signaled an incoming message. Her heart raced. It was from *True Story*. It was perfect timing. Here in New York City. Tyler was about to show her all of the sights that would soon become familiar to her when she worked for *True Story* as an intern. She and Tyler would see each other every day. Maybe meet for lunch in the middle of their work days. Everything was falling into place.

She clicked into the e-mail, and her heart sank. She read the dreaded form letter. *Thank you so much for your interest in our internship. We regret to inform you that we are unable to offer you a position. There were many talented writers who applied...*Her vision blurred as her eyes filled with tears, and she couldn't read the rest of the e-mail. *Now what?*

She sat on the bed. Her whole life seemed to swim around her, and she was sinking. She wanted to prove she could do this on her own, but she failed. Her head pounded as more tears fell. Her dream of New York faded as she realized where she was. She was *in* New

York. In the place where her dreams were dashed to pieces.

She'd be getting a tour of her dreams from Tyler, to see all the places she'd never see again. A tour of the life she'd failed to achieve. She looked in the mirror. Tears stained her shirt, and mascara slipped down her cheek.

She didn't want Tyler to know she was a failure. He'd been right that she put some of her own ambitions on hold, but she thought she could overcome that anyway. Why? Because she was a Montgomery. Winning was in the blood. And she wasn't going to be a failure. She'd tell him about her rejection after the conference.

She met Tyler downstairs in the lobby a few minutes later with flawless makeup.

"What's wrong?" Tyler's eyes searched hers.

"What do you mean?" Her puffy eyes were concealed. Liz smile felt too wide to feel genuine. She tried a smaller smile, but it felt just as forced.

She wanted to make the most of her two and half days touring New York before the conference. This might be the only chance she got to see the city. Now that she wouldn't be moving here.

The dimple disappeared from his cheek, concern laced his voice. "Something happened. You look deflated. What's wrong? Do you not like the room?" He looked like he might run to the front desk to demand a different one for her.

She put a hand on his forearm. "The room is perfect." As part of the VIP package she was in one of the presidential suites. She could feel moisture gathering at the corners of her eyes. None of her family members would have noticed her mood change. And that thought made her break down. She *had* to tell him. He would understand.

He slowly nodded. "Okay. What happened?"

They still had a few hours of light left. "Can we go walk while we talk?" Liz asked.

"Of course."

"I received a rejection letter from *True Story*," she said, once they were outside. She shrugged and pulled up her e-mail, showing him the two lines of text.

"This is addressed to E. Madison," he said.

"That's my pen name from high school journalism." She lowered her voice. "I don't want my name to be the reason I get a job." They seemed to walk in an aimless pattern up one street and down another. It felt like her life. Where was she going now? She followed Tyler's lead, unable to answer the question.

"I didn't pass the on-demand article part of the application. It was a broad topic, but I wrote it quickly. It was decent writing, but," she said, shrugging. "Not good enough. I can't believe I didn't check my e-mail on the computer to see the time stamp. I thought I had a full twelve hours to write it, and I had to cram it into twenty minutes." But that wasn't an excuse. Had her writing been better, twenty minutes should have been enough time, right?

"You could always resubmit under your real name," Tyler suggested.

"E. Madison is my real name, just not all of it. E is for Elizabeth, and Madison is my middle name."

"It's not the worst last name in the world to admit you're a Montgomery."

"It's not that. I just don't want that to be the reason I'm hired."

He looked at her for a long time. "Has that ever been the case before?"

She thought over high school, and Rick, and any time she was invited to a party where the invitation included Grip. "Probably."

"Well, you can't help that. You are who you are. You might get extra privileges, and you might not, but sometimes that's how life is."

"I know. I can't help but think if I'd have put more time into my article, or if I had taken a journalism job as a stepping stone to *True Story*, they would have accepted me. Instead, I took the easy way out and I've been helping my brother."

He squeezed her hand, reassuring her. "Sometimes we don't know what we don't know."

"Huh?"

"You made a decision. It's okay. Everything happens for a reason, and good can come out of painful experiences."

She took a deep breath. This was painful. And she had no backup plan. But maybe that was needed for the start of a new adventure. She thought of Ron when he tore his ACL and decided to end his football career. It hadn't been in his plan, but he did it. But she wasn't there yet. "Let's not dwell on this anymore. I'm okay. I want to enjoy myself while I'm here with you, and I want to see everything New York has to offer."

"Then I know where we should go next."

"Where?"

"You'll see."

Tyler pointed out different buildings, and architecture as they walked through the bustling streets. Smells from food trucks mingled with car exhaust, assaulted her senses, even in the cool air. She loved the feel of her hand in Tyler's, and soaked in everything, not knowing if she'd see it again for a long time.

Then he took her on a subway ride.

"Where are we going?" Liz said when they were back on the street again.

"Walking across the Brooklyn Bridge is one of my favorite things to do with people who come to visit New York. There's something about walking across it, toward the city."

Liz took in all of the views. The air, in contrast to the streets and subway, was fresh here, and calming. The noise of the city muffled through their entire walk. They took several pictures of each other and selfies together.

They entered the Financial District and soon stood at the base of the One World Trade Center. "I should have asked if you were scared of heights. You're not, are you?"

Liz looked up at the tallest building in New York City. It towered over everything around it. "Only when I'm jumping off. The high dive was never my favorite."

He squeezed her hand. "Want to go to the observatory? The view is breathtaking."

"Let's go."

Liz popped her ears several times in the ten seconds the elevator climbed to the top. The rush in her stomach felt like being on a rollercoaster ride. She was glad she was with Tyler.

"Wow," she said, when the presentation finished and the screens over the windows suddenly raised for them to see the New York skyline. "This is even better than the view flying in."

Tyler put an arm around her shoulders. "There's more to see."

They walked around the entire floor, and Tyler pointed out buildings, and bridges, naming each of them.

"There's the Statue of Liberty! It looks so small from here." She shoved the negative thoughts away that said she'd never see this view again. She could always come back to visit. And the view was breathtaking.

"We're up really high. It gives you an appreciation for how there is always something much bigger than ourselves."

It certainly did. Like maybe her problem of not getting the internship was much smaller when she saw the rest of the world surrounding her. She soaked it in, memorizing the colors and the shapes of the different buildings.

Tyler led her to the One Dine restaurant at the top. They enjoyed their meal, chatting about the day and then walked a final time around the observatory, taking in the

New York view at sunset. "The city has its charms," he said.

"Which city is more charming to live in? New York or Los Angeles?"

Tyler lifted an eyebrow and stole a glance at her. "I never mentioned living in Los Angeles." His lips curved ever so slightly.

"Google provided that golden nugget," she admitted.

"Ah, the wisdom of Google. See again the trouble with the famous lives we lead? No privacy at all." He winked at her. "Definitely New York."

"Are you excited about the conference?"

"Truthfully, I'm a little nervous."

"Ha. You're not." She had yet to see him really nervous, even when surrounded by strangers at the Kyle's football game, he seemed composed. His face said otherwise, so she added, "Nervous for what?"

"I'm the keynote, I get jittery before speaking."

"Do you? I wouldn't have pegged you for stage fright."

"More like the whole time at a conference, not just on the stage."

"Dig deeper, why is that?"

"Now, who's asking the hard questions?" His smile seemed forced.

"Believe it or not, I'm a little shy about success." He ran a hand through this hair. "I mean, lots of book signings break me out of being too shy, but I'm only with a reader for about thirty seconds, so it's not hard to be outgoing for a short time. But when you're at a conference, you're with the same people day in and out for the better part of a week.

"I want to be social with people, but I guess it boils down to everyone else having the advantage over me. Everyone knows me as Ty, so they think they're on a first name basis with me. I don't know their names, or anything about them, but they've read all of my books, can quote my bio, know my likes, my interests —everything."

Liz shrugged. "It's flattering, but I guess that's a little over the top. My family has gone through similar things. My broken engagement made headlines among football fans. It was crazy. But at least you have devoted fans in the mix."

"Fame is a double-edged sword. It's great to have people know you, and the perks are nice. It's rewarding to touch others' lives in a way that can't be done by just anyone, but at the same time it's..." He paused.

"Lonely? Isolating? Overbearing?"

He stared. "How do you know?"

Because I feel the same way. We're connected. She smiled. "Just because I'm not the one who's famous, doesn't mean I don't know what it feels like."

He nodded. "Of course."

"With my dad and brothers all superstars, you get used to feeling alone. I mean, not because they're famous and you're not, but more because the public life of an individual reaches to the family."

She looked out at the lights of the city against the darkening sky, taking a few pictures with her phone. "I wondered in high school which girls were really my friends, and which ones would hang out with me because I had an amazing twin brother—or three other older brothers. I *never* know if people like me for me." She took a breath. "It's one of the reasons I used my high school journalism penname when I first applied to *True Story*. I wanted them to see me for me, not who I'm related to."

"That makes sense. Don't worry." He squeezed her hand. "We can get you an interview with *True Story* this week. That will change their minds."

Liz smiled, hoping he knew how much she appreciated the offer. "Do you really think so? They are booked solid this week. I checked the schedule."

"I might be able to pull some strings."

"Thank you, Tyler." She wrapped her arms around his neck, drawing him closer to her and kissed him passionately, not caring who saw. Tyler wanted to help her reach her dreams. In that moment, she felt on top of the world.

CHAPTER EIGHTEEN

Tyler glanced over at Liz and smiled. Over the past two days they'd seen the New York Library, gone to a Broadway show, walked around Times Square, and toured through most of Central Park. But the memory of their kiss at the One World Trade Center two days ago, was still at the forefront of his mind. He wanted to kiss her again. He didn't want to stop kissing her. Heaven help him it would be a long conference this time, and he was in the mood to blow it off, and confess his love for her and kiss her again. And again. He shook his head as the taxi braked in the traffic.

They were almost to the conference, after having breakfast at his favorite restaurant at the other end of town. "Liz, how do you want this conference to work? Will you go off and do your own thing or do you want to attend classes together?"

Liz tilted her head. "I haven't really thought about it. Do you have a preference?"

"This is your first conference. Sometimes it's helpful to shadow someone else. Other times it's nice to break off and attend separately."

"I'll follow your lead on this. I already feel like an intruder."

Tyler reached for her hand. "I hope that's not really how you feel. This is one of the best conferences to attend. But, we are going to run into an awkward question. We should figure out the answer before it comes up."

She raised her eyebrows as the taxi pulled up to the conference center.

"I talk with so many people, and if you are with me..." Tyler hesitated. He didn't want Liz's perspective on fame to dampen this conference. *This shouldn't be a hard conversation.* He wanted to know where they stood.

"I'll be in your way for networking."

"No. Not at all. But I have to know how to introduce you. I mean, if I introduce you as the sister of the star I'm writing a biography about, and then we are at the gala together, it will look like I haven't been telling the whole story."

Understanding dawned on her face, and a small smile curled one side of her lips. "Ty Lake. I thought you were supposed to be good with words. If you want me to be your girlfriend, you didn't have to make up a long-winded reason for asking."

Tyler's heart pounded a little harder. "So, you don't hate the idea?"

Liz kissed him quickly as the valet opened her door. "I definitely don't hate the idea."

The ballroom was lined with rows of chairs. He motioned for her to keep walking, but she stopped several rows from where he was headed.

"I want you to meet some people before we take our seats," Tyler said. He headed toward his agent, Alex, who was texting furiously on his phone. Alex's dark hair was cropped short, and he wore a dark gray suit.

Alex shook hands with Tyler. "Good to see you." Alex turned to Liz, raising his eyebrows. "And this is..."

Tyler made the introduction.

"It's a pleasure to finally meet you." Alex took Liz's hand and kissed the back of it.

Liz blushed, and Tyler's jaw muscle refused to relax. Alex's job revolved around charming people, and he was good at it. But he knew Liz wouldn't appreciate that kind of attention. He put an arm around her shoulders protectively, though he didn't think he needed to stake his claim in front of Alex. But just in case.

Alex cleared his throat. "Glad I caught you this morning. Slight change of plans for me. I have a conference call for the next hour, but I'll catch up with you later."

Tyler nodded, and they wound their way to their seats near the front.

Tyler watched in awe as Liz sat beside him on their Wednesday night dinner after a full day of classes. He'd spent three days at this conference with an amazing woman he now called his girlfriend. A weekend of sightseeing with her was the most fun he'd had in New York in a long time. She loved discovering new places, and learning the rich history and culture. And he loved it more because he was with her.

He didn't realize originally what a significant role Liz would play in setting the tone of his nerves during the conference. She was perfectly at ease as she ate the formal dinner, chatting politely with the other conference attendees at their table. An evening speaker would start up halfway through the main course, but right now they were still on salads and breads.

Between classes they had talked about their relationship. How would Kyle react to Tyler dating Liz? They'd have a few weeks before the Happy Moments charity ball and the family Thanksgiving dinner to figure out how to tell her family. Tyler smiled at the thought, and then was drawn back into the conversation around him, staring at Liz's lips again.

Liz nudged him, whispering as she dabbed her lips with her napkin, "Do I have something in my teeth?"

He shook his head, then he leaned his head so his mouth grazed her ear as he spoke. "No. Just distracted by your lips. You have very kissable lips, you know."

Liz colored slightly, and glanced around the table. "I didn't know, but it's still rude to stare."

Tyler addressed a portly man in a colored shirt and matching striped tie across the table. "George, have you met Liz yet? Liz is my girlfriend and wants to write for *True Story*. She agreed to accompany me for the entire week of classes, if you can imagine."

"Ah, she must love you to do that." George winked at Liz.

"Liz, this is George and Julie Hanover. They are on the board for this conference, and spend a lot of their time preparing for these events. We're lucky to have them."

Julie laughed. "Yes, we met her earlier. Liz is a dear." She and George were good people, going out of their way to meet new people.

"A pleasure meeting both of you, again." Liz smiled.

"Liz, didn't you say you were writing something? What genre are you dabbling in?" Julie's voice was kind, always genuinely interested in others.

Tyler waited for Liz's response. He knew she wanted to write for *True Story*, but was there more?

She met his gaze, and tilted her head before she addressed Julie. "Yes, dabbling is definitely the right word for how I write. It's more of a lengthy outline and lots of notes for chapters than an actual story. But it's a middle-grade fantasy, just something I started in high school."

Tyler's eyes widened? How did he not know this about Liz? Why would she keep this from him?

"So, you write in the same genre as Ty then. I bet he's a good asset." Julie pointed her fork in Tyler's direction.

Liz cleared her throat. "Tyler, uh, Ty, writes in so many different genres, and I'm not that broad, but he is definitely the best asset to have around."

Nice recovery, Tyler thought.

"Yes, but he started his career writing middle-grade fantasy," Julie said.

Tyler jumped in. "That's true I did. Published my first one in high school. And it's still one of my favorite genres to write, even as I have expanded to YA and adult fiction, and now non-fiction with the biography."

Julie nodded. The next course came out and small talk wandered to the day's events and the classes. Julie gave several suggestions to Liz about what classes to take for the middle-grade genre. As he sat there listening politely, all he could think about was being alone with Liz.

After the evening of mingling and signing books, Tyler walked with Liz to the elevator.

"You're one popular guy, Mr. Ty Lake."

"It's embarrassing sometimes," he confessed.

"Ah, you're used to it by now, no need for the false modesty. It's great how you take time for people and make them feel valued when you sign their books."

"Thanks." He was stunned. Had she seen that in him with the books he signed?

They stepped inside the open elevator door. His brow furrowed as he remembered Liz had kept her writing of a novel to herself. How was he going to bring that up?

"So, what's wrong?" Liz asked quietly.

"I thought you were only wanting to write for *True Story*. I didn't know you're pursuing fiction too."

"I wasn't keeping it from you. I'm majored in English remember, and when you asked me about coming, I was mostly thinking about *True Story*, but," she said, shrugging, "I don't know. So many authors and writers were talking about fiction during one of the first classes, I started thinking of this old manuscript. Besides what I've written down is hardly worthy to be called 'writing.' Mostly they are thoughts, and outlines. A few paragraphs here, a few pages of dialogue there. I wrote it a long time ago, and haven't pulled it out since high school."

His brows softened. "I wish I would have known. I mean, all day long I've been introducing you as my girl-friend, and your dream to write for *True Story*."

Her face colored. "My dream is to write for *True Story*, and I like the title of your girlfriend. The classes today were advanced on a fiction level, but I learned in them. I just didn't have anything to apply it to, until I thought of this old novel."

The elevator door opened onto her floor, and Tyler walked her to her door.

"Maybe tomorrow you can pick your own schedule, and we can see each other during meals, if we don't end up going to the same classes," he suggested. She would come away from the conference with a better experience if she picked the classes that applied to her right now.

Her face lit up. "Are you sure you can handle being in a class without me there to ward off the eager girls vying for your attention?" Amusement sparkled in her eyes.

"I didn't notice any of that today," Tyler said. He'd been completely focused on her.

"That's because I was there giving them all the evil eye when they started checking you out." She laughed, and gave him a hug. "Are you sure you wouldn't mind?"

"No, I want you to make the most out of this conference." He smiled, then kissed her soundly.

CHAPTER NINETEEN

The next morning, Liz waited in the hotel lobby for Tyler. She pulled out her schedule, looking at the day's events.

"Good morning," he said over her shoulder.

"Well, hello." Her stomach fluttered in all different directions at the sound of his voice. She stood to greet him.

Tyler's hug and kiss melted her. He held her in his arms longer than she expected, but she didn't mind. The warmth filled her.

"I have some good news for you," he said, sitting next to her on the plush loveseat.

"Oh?"

"I talked with *True Story*. They would like to meet with you during the gala."

She squealed with excitement. "That's wonderful. Thank you, Tyler." Maybe she'd be calling New York home after all. *True Story,* New York, Tyler. Everything was falling into place.

She angled her head and kissed him. Her hand moved to his cheek, feeling the beginnings of his scruff. She was lost in his kiss until two loud clicks were accompanied by bright lights.

She cringed, knowing exactly what it meant. Maybe a writing career was just as invasive as a football one.

Tyler drew his gaze away from hers and scanned in the direction of the lights, watching as one of the conference photographers moved away.

Tyler grabbed Liz's hand and walked toward the retreating figure. "Peter. Wait up."

A man turned, a lazy smile on his face.

"What do you think you are doing?" Tyler folded his arms across his chest.

"Catching writers in action." Peter smiled, obviously pleased with his play on words.

Tyler raised a single eyebrow. "You think you can interrupt me in *action*, and walk away like it's no big deal?"

"I didn't want to interrupt."

"It's a little late for that." Tyler's eyes landed on Peter's camera.

"Play nice, Tyler, or you won't see what the camera caught." Peter tapped his lens.

"Ah, and what was that?"

"I'd say if a picture is worth roughly 1,000 words, I've got at least 10,000 to tell your little love story that is blossoming here." Peter pointed his camera between Tyler and Liz.

The two men burst out laughing, giving each other a back-slapping hug.

"Good to see you, Peter." Tyler slapped his back again.

"You too, Tyler."

Tyler? Not Ty? Old friend from outside the writing world, maybe?

"Hand over the camera, and nobody gets hurt," Tyler said with a mischievous grin.

"Take a look." Peter held out his camera, while keeping his other hand in a surrender pose.

Tyler's smile broadened as he scrolled through the pictures. "Send these to me, will you?"

"Done. And should I send you a copy as well?" Peter turned to Liz.

She cleared her throat. "I'm sure Tyler will send me copies as soon as he gets them."

Peter rubbed the back of his neck and sighed. "Okay, only if Tyler promises to send them to you the moment he gets them."

Tyler's eyes gleamed. "A promise I can keep."

Peter nodded, and then disappeared around a corner.

"You must know him well," she said.

"Peter was a college buddy of mine. We worked on the college paper together. When I would interview someone for a story, he'd always interrupt my interview to take the picture. I'd pretend to get mad, but he inter-rupted at the precise moment to get the perfect shot."

Tyler put his arm on the small of Liz's back. "Let's get to class."

Liz spun in her midnight blue gown in front of the mirror as she got ready for Friday's gala. The rhinestone detail would sparkle under the spotlights in the ballroom. She brushed a few stray curls away from her eyes, glad that the softening cream she applied tamed her curls in the humid air in New York. Without it she'd be the human equivalent of a Chia pet.

She relived the last few days of classes, workshops and networking with Tyler. She'd had an incredible week.

A knock at the door drew her out of the memory. Tyler grinned as she opened the door.

"You're stunning," he said.

And you're sexy. Tyler was the complete package in his tailored tux, bowtie, and cuff links. Her breath caught. He'd make a handsome groom. Her cheeks heated at that thought. "You're not half bad yourself!"

"Shall we?" He held out his arm.

She took his arm, then reached on her tiptoes, planting a passionate kiss on his lips, and whispered, "For luck on your speech." Then, replacing her heels on the ground, she added, "Let's go."

"If I realized what luck I'd get before a speech, I'd have signed up for more speeches weeks ago."

Liz squeezed his arm. "You wish."

"Yes, I do. Maybe next time I have a speech you'll be by my side again."

"It's a high possibility. After all, I'm introducing you at the Happy Moments charity ball."

Tyler raised his eyebrows to her. "But you wouldn't object to another one of these evenings? A writing speech."

"With you dressed up? Naw. I could take a few more of them," she said as they approached the elevator.

Tyler leaned closer to her as they stared at the closed door ahead of them. "Were you just being coy, or would you really like more evenings like this?"

She felt heat creep up her neck. "I would like more evenings like *this*." She swept her hand with a flourish to include their dressy state. "But more specifically, I'd like more evenings like *this*." She squeezed his arm entwined with hers.

She didn't even have time to breathe before he kissed her, his lips insistent. The wait for the elevator didn't seem long enough. Someone cleared their throat. Tyler pulled back, and squeezed her fingers. He bent low to her ear. "Looks like the elevator is here," he whispered, and she opened her eyes.

Several other people were in the elevator, the open door allowing a perfect view of their kiss.

She held onto his arm in the crook of his elbow, and smiled. "Definitely more evenings like *that*," she whispered as they settled into the middle of the elevator. His mouth curved upward. It was the perfect start to a wonderful night.

CHAPTER TWENTY

Tyler was grateful Liz was comfortable with extravagant parties. The gala was a major event, and she seemed right at home as they socialized. She put others at ease, and charmed them without awkwardness. She talked with agents and publishers and writers, and the more he watched her, the deeper he felt for her.

She hadn't shied away from his questions about pursuing their relationship further. And that's what he wanted. He was proud of her for choosing to attend other classes that interested her. She wasn't the clingy type who followed him around like a little puppy.

She was able to pursue her own ideas, and do it independently. He admired that. Yet, at the same time he missed her when she wasn't sitting next to him in the classes. He sighed. She was perfect for him.

"Tyler, darling." Liz's voice came through to him, and she gave him a questioning look. "They were wondering about your latest work after the biography. I told them I was sworn to secrecy, but do you have any tidbits you'd like to impart to them yourself?" There was a twinkle in her eye. She didn't have a clue about his current work in progress, aside from the biography.

He squeezed her hand. "Prepare for something you haven't seen before from me. But you'll like it." He gave a winning smile to the crowd, and Tyler led her away.

"I can't wait to see what you have in store," she said.

"Me too." He smiled. "It's getting there, but it's different. Thankfully I am working on a few projects at once, so I can bounce around."

"Sounds daring."

"A little. But if my newest idea doesn't pan out, I've got a few other things that won't be delayed by my dabbling in a new genre."

Her eyebrows rose. "I'm intrigued. Do I get a sneak peek?"

He shook his head, then stopped. "Maybe I could arrange that. It's top secret."

"I'm good at keeping secrets."

"Maybe after we get back from your extended Thanksgiving weekend."

"That's a long time to keep me in suspense."

Tyler squeezed her hand, and leaned toward her. "I'm a writer. You'll have to get used to suspense."

"After Thanksgiving? I like the sound of that." Her face pinked as she looked down.

He squeezed their entwined fingers again, enjoying the feel of her hand in his own. It was a perfect fit.

A group of people mingled toward the back of the room. "There's the group from *True Story*. They're expecting you. I'll introduce you, but I'm not staying while you meet with them."

Tyler talked and signed autographs, while keeping an eye on Liz. He hoped the meeting was going well. He knew how she felt about networking, but meeting *True Story* at the conference would be a step in her favor.

She shook the hands of everyone she'd been talking with, then headed toward the refreshment tables on the outskirts of the room. He caught up to her. "Did you have a good meeting?" He had a twinkle in his eye.

"I did. They seemed to know a lot more about me than I was prepared for. They already knew E. Madison and Liz Montgomery were the same person. Perhaps a famous epic fantasy author filled them in?" She took his arm and they walked toward the center of the room.

"They seemed interested. Are you mad?" He hoped she wasn't mad. E. Madison wasn't registered as a conference guest, so he had explained to *True Story*.

She shook her head. "Thank you."

"After all, you can't put your dreams on hold forever. You need to go after them."

"I'll go after them in my own time." Her tone sounded defensive.

He turned her toward him, keeping his hands around her waist. "Liz. You're a great cheerleader in your family.

The best. But don't you think it's time to focus on you? Don't you think it's time to let your dreams come true?"

"And you think *True Story* is my answer?"

"If you think it is, then yes. You're talented. You're amazing, and you can still cheer others in your family on, even if you pursue your own career. You don't have to keep working for Kyle in Happy Moments."

"He can't do it without me." She sighed. She looked defeated, but he wanted to empower her.

"He'll manage. But he doesn't even know that you don't like it. Give others some more credit. If you were honest with him about it, he'd understand. He wants your happiness, too. It's not just about creating happy moments for others, it's about letting yourself have happy moments."

Liz bit her lip and nodded slowly.

"If it were me, I wouldn't let the fear of letting others down stop me from doing what is best for me."

"I'll think about that. *True Story* asked for an interview early tomorrow morning before my flight. They'd like to go through a few things. They haven't given away all of the internships yet."

"You should do it."

"I will."

CHAPTER TWENTY-ONE

Liz licked the spoon of her caramel dessert one last time, savoring the flavor, then pushed the dessert plate aside. She was thankful that her gown wasn't so tight it pinched her stomach although dinner was filling.

"How was it?" Tyler asked. He had opted for a layered chocolate cake.

"Delicious. Yours?"

"Not as good as watching you enjoy your dessert, but good." He raised his eyebrows, a teasing look in his eyes. "I'm about to be announced. I need to get backstage."

Liz gave him a kiss. "Good luck. I'm all ears!"

She took a sip of her water as Alex returned to the table after taking a call. "You missed out. Dinner was good. Dessert was better."

Alex looked to Liz. "Where's Ty? I have great news for both of you. Skipping food was worth it."

Liz's eyebrows raised. "He's backstage, about to be announced. Do share."

A server brought a plate of food and roll to Alex's place, and Alex thanked him for holding the meal.

"I just worked out a huge publicity tour for him. We're talking more than the usual book signings and TV spots, and he'll also do social media broadcasts from some iconic places. So far, I've set three of those, though there are a few more."

"Sounds exciting." *But I'd prefer to hear about it after Tyler's speech.*

Tyler was announced and took the mic after a generous round of applause. Alex's grin widened, and he whispered, "You'll be happy to know that Tyler working on your brother's biography has been a huge win for Tyler. His stardom pulls a lot of weight. Not that Tyler can't get his own publicity without Kyle's help, but there were some extra bonuses thrown in when I name-dropped who Tyler was writing a biography for."

Liz nodded politely, concentrating on Tyler, not Alex.

"And of course, I have you to thank for a lot of it, too." He gestured to her, and ate another bite of his filet mignon.

She tilted her head. "Oh?"

Alex took a drink then wiped his mouth. "At first I was wondering why he was wasting all of his precious writing time working on the charity. After all, Tyler has never been interested in that type of thing before. Of course, he felt obligated to help you. Who wouldn't. I mean, you're beautiful, and Tyler has a thing for redheads, and his biography would have been delayed or canceled if he didn't.

"But once he told me the amount of publicity it would gain him, I started going to work on our other contacts. This cross-over idea is the perfect way to bring in extra advertising while he launches his new series. With any luck, he won't have to waste his time doing charity work again with the amount of revenue this one brings in."

Liz raised a hand to her furrowed brow. She felt drenched with a bucket of cold water. She tried to focus on Tyler's speech, but Alex's words of Tyler feeling obligated and only caring about the advertising echoed loudly in her ears.

She stared through her empty plate. Every memory with Tyler bombarded her senses. What had he said the first time he agreed to help her? That he wanted to help? She assumed he meant he wanted to help *her*, but it was all for himself.

The sparks were there between them, she felt it, but perhaps it was one more lie. The kissing was a lie. His plans for the future after the gala were a lie. A fire burned inside of her.

"His launch will happen before Thanksgiving," Alex spoke over Tyler's speech as he ate. "We'll push hard until mid-November on more PR, and then he'll be back to New York, before touring for two weeks before Thanksgiving. Everything is lined up. His checkmate will happen."

I've been a pawn. Liz drew in a sharp breath and looked at Tyler. He was so collected. She doubted he ever felt uncomfortable in front of a crowd.

Alex's phone buzzed on the table next to him. He looked at the screen, and stood. "I've got to take this. They're working overtime for him. Now that he saved the day in solving your charity problems, we can all focus on his career. It's a relief for him to have this charity mess behind him." He left the table, phone up to his ear.

This mess. It felt like a mess. *Could it be true? Is Alex right—is this whole thing fake?* Liz blinked rapidly. She was in a formal gown. She was at the front of the room. She wouldn't make a scene.

Tyler had just told her that she shouldn't be concerned about others' feelings when making the best decision about her career. She thought he'd been talking about her life, and her family's circumstances. But had he really been talking about his choice?

Had he been hinting that she should change her way of dealing with the charity, to make himself feel better about blowing them off, because it was better for *his* career? Her head swam as the last several weeks came into view through this new lens of information.

He helped me on the charity because it was best for him—not me. Now that he has his tour set up, that's the priority, not his commitment to Happy Moments. We can both go our separate ways. Her breaths came in rapid, shallow successions.

Tyler knew the planned schedule, so why hadn't he mentioned that he was going to be touring during the charity ball? He was the keynote speaker for the event. She only had a few weeks to replace him. How could he do this to her?

This was a Rick situation all over again. Well not quite the same. Her relationship with Tyler hadn't gotten as serious as Rick's, and they weren't engaged, but there was one major difference that set them apart. She'd need longer to get over the heartbreak that was Tyler Lakewood.

As Tyler told a joke, she brushed a tear from her eye. She hadn't heard a word he said. She looked in his direction, but saw nothing.

The moment he ended, and the applause started, she took the clutch purse off the table. She needed to make her exit before Tyler came back. She spotted a side door, and followed a server through when it opened. Applause continued as the swinging door closed behind her.

She turned around, realizing she was in the serving kitchen area. Not good. A pain shot through her, knowing she had looked forward to this night since the first time Tyler mentioned it. She forced a smile, and brushed another tear from her eye.

"Miss, you can't come through this way." A female voice called to her. "The exit for the banquet is at the back of the room. The side doors are only for the staff."

Liz bit her bottom lip. She couldn't wind through all of the tables in the banquet hall unnoticed. *Could this moment get any worse?*

A woman's hand caught hers as she was about to

push the swinging door outward. "Miss, are you okay?" The dark-haired server looked at her with kind eyes.

Liz started to nod her head, but ended up shaking it.

The server pulled her hand. "Follow me, I'll take you the back way." She squeezed Liz's arms lightly, and the memories of hanging on Tyler's arm through the entire evening swam across her mind, spilling onto her face in a rush of tears. They hadn't even danced together. Not that she cared now. Waste of a perfectly good dress. She wound through several food prep stations and past other servers who gave her questioning glances, but didn't say anything.

They reached a door, and the server paused before saying softly, "There's a maintenance elevator outside this door. It will take you to your floor, right next to the laundry facilities when you come out." She looked at Liz once more, bit her lip, and then grabbed Liz in a hug. "I hope you feel better. You look like the belle of the ball." And with that she disappeared back into the madness of servers cleaning dishes and sorting napkins.

Once in her room, Liz pulled off her heels. She eyed the clock. It was late.

She packed quickly. The mingling and networking continued until midnight or after. She needed to leave before Tyler came to find her. She couldn't face him. She quickly wrote a note to him on the hotel stationery, explaining she left early to go see her brother's game. It was partially true. She wouldn't miss Grip's game tomorrow because of Tyler. She wrote instructions for the front desk to deliver the note to Tyler in the morning.

She reached for the hotel phone to call the front desk for a cab.

～

She took a quick flight from JFK to Atlanta. The four-hour layover had been exhausting, but it was the only solution her airline could offer her that would have her leaving on an earlier flight.

She blinked hard, her eyelids heavy, as she adjusted to the bright florescent cabin lights. She deflated the neck pillow she bought from the kiosk before boarding and rubbed her neck, attempting to work out the sore muscles.

The morning sun filtered through the clouds. The harsh contrast made it look like they'd get a hard rain storm in the next few hours. Liz looked through her purse, trying to find a piece of gum or a mint to get rid of her morning breath.

The plane pulled into the gate in Denver, and a high-pitched ding announced the ability to unfasten her seat-belt. She pulled her suitcase down from the bin, stumbling from the weight in her exhausted arms. She slung her purse higher on her shoulder, and pushed the suitcase in front of her.

There were only a few people waiting at the gate across from them. She glanced around the airport and then stopped herself when she realized who she was looking for. Tyler wouldn't be here.

∾

On the way home, she took her phone off airplane mode. Alerts and texts buzzed, and she remembered she'd blown off *True Story*'s interview this morning. In her anger at Tyler she'd completely forgotten. There went her chances. It was fine. She'd find somewhere else to apply. Maybe on the west coast, away from Tyler.

Liz walked into her house. The drive from Denver to Boulder had taxed all her mental ability. Which was good. Because it kept her mind off Tyler, and how mad she was at him.

Coco and Jenny sat on the couch, eating yogurt parfaits. Mandy stretched on the floor, her arms reaching toward the parfait positioned next to one of her feet.

"Hi," Liz said.

"Hey! We weren't expecting you back until super late tonight." Jenny jumped up and gave her a hug. "How'd you get here so early?"

"I took an earlier flight."

Jenny studied her face. "Coco, whip out the ice cream. Liz has some explaining."

"Oh, good. The parfait is fine if we really want to be healthy. But I'll take sundaes for breakfast any day." Coco took out a few pints of ice cream, and some glass bowls and set them on the counter. "Mandy, are you in for some ice cream?"

Mandy glanced up at Liz. "I'm in."

"Thanks guys," Liz said. "I'm so exhausted. Red-eyes are not my preferred travel time."

"Why did you switch?" Coco asked.

"I'm assuming that's why we're having sundaes for breakfast today," Jenny said.

Coco brought over the sundaes and placed the one drowning in caramel in front of Liz.

With two cherries. Yep. If the retelling of the story made her sick, the sugar would douse the pain. "Thanks."

"Don't thank me yet. Spill it."

So, she did. In between bites of her Salted Caramel Core ice cream she told them about Tyler. She left nothing out, holding her roommates' attention so well they each ignored their sundaes, leaving puddles of melted ice cream in the bowls. Emotions swirled around her like the caramel in her ice cream. She'd need a lot more caramel to get over Tyler.

"What are you going to do now?" Mandy asked.

Liz shrugged. "There's nothing really to do." She wouldn't repeat another Rick mistake.

"But you'll be seeing him again for the Happy Moments charity ball in a few weeks."

"His agent has other plans for him that week. He won't be there." *Besides I don't want him there. I hate being used.* "I'll need to find someone else to announce the summer project."

"You could do it."

"I'll do it." But as she said it, her stomach twisted in knots. Maybe it was the sugar, but she had given a draft speech to Tyler, and hadn't thought of it since. "Or maybe I can find someone else to announce the summer project." But her mind drew a blank.

"He's your brother's biographer. You'll run into him sooner or later."

Liz nodded, numb to the obvious. And yet, it couldn't matter. It *didn't* matter. "You're right, he's Kyle's biographer. And that's all he is. Sure, we had fun together for a few weeks, but it's over now."

A text popped up on Liz's phone from Tyler. She closed the app without reading it. By now he'd have received her message from the front desk. Her roommates watching her so she turned over her phone so the screen faced down on the table.

"That can't be how you really feel," Mandy said soothingly.

Liz's heart cracked. She needed numbness to take over. This pain was worse than breaking her femur.

Later that afternoon, Liz cheered for Grip at his game. The stadium held so many memories, but today the only ones that screamed at her over the cheering crowd were the memories of Tyler. Their first meeting replayed in her mind, and she could almost feel the sticky root beer on her arms and Tyler's firm grip around her. Then Tyler's face when Sam finished laughing at her for flirting with the guy he wanted to introduce her to. She was so distracted by the memories she cheered for the wrong team when they scored a touchdown.

Tyler's texts and phone calls kept her phone constantly buzzing, and she finally turned it off. Except to let him know she arrived home, there was no reason to talk to him right now.

She pushed the memories away harder, but the pull from Tyler felt too strong. She was attracted to him. She'd fallen hard for him. She admired the way he wrote, but her brain was scrambled when she thought about his words. She wasn't over him. Not by a long shot. But there'd be time for that. For all intents and purposes, he had been right. She *had* put her dreams on hold, and she did it purposefully.

Cheering for Grip felt mechanical. She had assumed cheering was an important part of her brothers' success, but they didn't need her to do it. They would have been just as successful without her putting her dreams on hold for them. It wasn't something she'd have to pick between either. She could have pursued her own dreams at the same time she cheered for her brothers. Why hadn't she done that?

A weight formed in the bottom of her stomach. Tyler had been right about her. And what if her dream to get away to New York and write for *True Story* didn't happen? She tried to please her brother by letting him think Happy Moments was her dream too, but that wasn't where her heart was. If *True Story* didn't pan out, would she be stuck cheering and helping others get their happy moments for the rest of her life? It had never seemed like a terrible option. Until now.

Play after play she cheered for Grip and his team-mates, but her heart wasn't in it, and her brain focused on the fool she'd been with Tyler. His words of encouragement to follow her dreams and stop being the cheerleader replayed over and over in her mind. Maybe Tyler had been talking about himself during that too, but she needed to figure out what she wanted in life. It was time for her to take a serious look at her goals and dreams.

CHAPTER TWENTY-TWO

Tyler paced his New York apartment. The view overlooked Central Park. Normally it was a calming sight. He left another voicemail on Liz's phone. How many times was he going to leave the same message?

She texted back once to let him know that she made it safely back to Colorado. But she hadn't returned his calls. He was baffled. He thought back to the last night of the Digital Quill Conference. He'd been smitten all week long. And longer.

He racked his brain for answers as he stared at his laptop screen. Maybe it had been a bad idea to pull some strings at *True Story* for her interview. He thought she'd appreciate the gesture, but she had mentioned several times she didn't like using others' connections. She hadn't seemed too bugged about it, but maybe she was.

He was an idiot. He'd done exactly what she'd told him not to do.

After his speech, he had looked for her, but had assumed she turned in early, since she had an early interview then long flight the next morning. Alex didn't know where she went, and Tyler had headed toward the door to find her, but was caught for the next hour in conversations and mingling.

He had knocked lightly on her door, not wanting to wake her if she was already asleep. She hadn't answered, and he wasn't too surprised. But the next morning he received a note from the front desk, informing him that Liz had checked out the night before. Some excuse about wanting to get back to watch Grip's game. As he read the words over and over they sounded hollow.

After spending almost every day talking and being together to work on the charity, not seeing her while he had been in Texas before the writer's conference had felt like living in a desert without water. Their time together in New York had given him an oasis. And he drank it in. Of course, he knew that her primary motivation would be the conference and the networking it provided. But was that her only reason for coming with him? Had their whole relationship been a mirage?

She'd been excited to come out early and spend time with him for two days before the conference began, but was that only because she had never been to New York and wanted a tour?

He was a fool if he thought bugging her everyday would change her mind about him, but hadn't there been a connection between them? Their kissing would say yes.

The way she flirted would say yes, so why the radio silence for the last few days?

Maybe she was trying to catch up on her school work. She had put a lot of it on hold to redo the Happy Moments summer project plan. That was probably it. She needed to catch up. He didn't want to be a distraction. He could be patient. They hadn't really talked about the way this long-distance relationship would work. And he was going to be swamped with the itinerary Alex threatened to keep him busy with from now until the new year.

Realization dawned on him. Had it been his conversation about following her dreams that had hurt her feelings? Maybe she was bugged at him for speaking so bluntly about it. But he couldn't not share his thoughts. He'd interviewed and shadowed her family, and he knew that she was making major sacrifices for them to the detriment of her own career.

She was loyal, and he admired that, but he knew that supporting others didn't mean you had to sacrifice everything either. It was a balancing act. Maybe he'd been out of line. He'd only known her family for a few months. That didn't make him an expert on the situation. Maybe he offended her. But it was worth the risk.

He wanted her to know that she could follow her dreams, and still support her brothers' dreams at the same time. Maybe he was justifying his own behavior since he didn't have a large family to sacrifice for. Maybe he'd have done the exact same thing Liz had done if he were in her shoes. Had he made her feel that supporting her family had been a waste of her skills and talents? The idea weighed on him. He needed to apologize.

There was a knock at the door.

"Alex? What are you doing here? I thought we were meeting this afternoon." Tyler motioned for Alex to come in, and he sat in the middle of the couch, spreading out documents on top of the coffee table.

"We need to go over your schedule for the next month, and I've got a lunch date that might go all afternoon."

Tyler wiped a hand across his face. "Okay. Show me your ideas."

"Here's what I've lined up," Alex said, handing him a paper and shuffling a few others around.

"You mean, this is what you're considering," he said, looking over the exhaustive schedule.

Alex shook his head. "No. This is the exciting news I wanted to tell you on Saturday. This *is* the schedule. It took me all of last week to finalize the details, but this is it. Isn't it great? Lots of publicity before and during your launch."

Tyler looked through the weeks. He would have no time to write. This would push Kyle's biography out by at least three months. He scanned down through the traveling. Most of the flights were direct, but he'd be living out of a suitcase and eating airport food for weeks back to back. "You scheduled me for three weeks solid surrounding Thanksgiving?"

"It's the only way we could make all of your guest

appearances. I threw in the book signings wherever you were having an interview. It's fairly standard."

"I told you I already have plans for Thanksgiving."

"And I have Thanksgiving Day open for you."

"I need the weekend before. I'm a keynote at the Happy Moments charity ball."

"Now that you have a morning show and three other events that day, I'm sure they'll understand."

Liz was counting on him to be there. He wouldn't let her down. "The charity ball will be packed with big donors."

"Donors to a charity, not to you." Alex waved his hand in the air like he was shooing away a pesky fly. "We have a tight schedule to keep everything on the list."

"Rearrange the list. I need that Saturday off."

"Is this about that redhead? Lily?"

"Liz."

"Whatever. Is it?"

"I've made a commitment to be there. It's for Kyle's charity. I'm writing his biography. I'm not going to bail for an unimportant signing. Kyle is counting on me. And yes. Liz is counting on me too."

"She didn't seem too bothered by it when I told her how much you'd be traveling." Alex flipped through a few more papers. "Here's the plan for your appearance in Los Angeles. There's still extra time to add in two more bookstores if you want to, or you can stay here during your whole stay." He pointed to a map with dots all around it.

Tyler froze. "You talked to Liz about my schedule before I approved it?"

Alex rubbed thumb and index finger together before looking up. "I may have mentioned it when I got back to the table. You were already backstage. I had to tell *somebody* the good news—and she was the only one around. Besides I gave you this same schedule the day before your speech. You had no objections then."

"Glancing over ideas didn't mean I gave permission." Tyler scrubbed his hand over his face. "You told her I'd be traveling over Thanksgiving?"

"I showed her the paper with some notes on it. She may have seen that."

Tyler threw up his hands. "Alex. You're skating on thin ice. I like this girl. A lot. You all but told her I'm blowing her off. Without my permission. I'm not agreeing to this schedule." No wonder Liz wasn't returning his calls.

"I've already made plans."

"Unmake them." He held Alex's gaze, unblinking.

Alex fidgeted. "I'm not making any promises. This schedule took me hours to set up. Rescheduling will be difficult."

"You'll figure it out." Tyler stepped toward his apartment door, holding it open for Alex. "And next time, don't schedule my calendar without clearing the dates with me first."

Alex finally looked a little sheepish. "Sorry."

"You'll be sorrier if I can't fix this with Liz."

CHAPTER TWENTY-THREE

L iz went straight to Kyle's office when she arrived at his house the night before the charity ball. With her family bustling around, and Kandice helping get everyone settled, Liz hoped she could slip away unnoticed. Grip had invited Cassie to come for the week, and seeing her here made her miss Tyler all over again, and a fresh wave of anger that he chose to bail on the charity ball. She told herself it was to talk to Kyle, and not to get away from the nagging thought that Tyler wasn't here.

She closed the door softly behind her, waiting by the door. Kyle turned around, pointed to the phone he held up to his ear, but motioned her forward. She took a seat, and listened to the end of his phone call.

Kyle stood and gave her a hug. "You're just the person I wanted to see."

"Oh? I'm ready for tomorrow's speech. Did you want a run-through?"

"Tyler decided to pass the buck back to you, did he?"

Liz chewed on her lip. "Not exactly. I assumed since he was back to back with his own PR for the last two weeks, I'd give him the out. I let him know I could take care of it. His agent was super clear that he didn't have time for it anyway."

An e-mail alert came through Liz's phone. She looked down at her phone in her hands, and saw it was from Tyler. She rolled her eyes. It could wait.

Kyle's eyes squinted at her. "Was that Tyler? He mentioned he was having a hard time getting a hold of you."

Liz shrugged. Tyler had sent flowers, caramel chocolates, and then edible flower arrangements. Her roommates had enjoyed them. She wasn't going to be bought off by someone she loved, who used her.

Kyle moved to sit in the chair next to Liz's. "I don't want to get in the middle of you and Tyler. But he hasn't told me that he is canceling his keynote address, so as far as I know he's still planning on it."

Liz's heart raced at that revelation. "I'm ready in case he doesn't show."

"Is this going to be too hard for you to have him here tomorrow? Say the word, and we'll figure something else out."

"You'd do that for *me*?"

"You're my only sister, Liz. That's what family does. You can count on me for anything."

Her shoulder slumped as she pushed further into the chair. "I guess I wanted to see if he would choose me, er, the charity, over the schedule that he had. He didn't tell me that he was double booked when he agreed to speak." *Or that he only wanted the publicity when he helped me.* That one still stung. Maybe there was another way to look at it. She hoped she was wrong.

Kyle's eyes softened. "You don't know what choice he is going to make."

"He should have told his agent he already had something this weekend."

"Don't hold that against him."

"Don't you?"

"No. I don't. He's not that kind of person. Agents, public relations, sports channels. They all have their own agendas. Sometimes things are double booked."

"You're not going to fire him as your biographer?"

Kyle studied her with serious eyes. "Is that what you want me to do?"

She shook her head. "No," she said softly.

"I picked him to do a job for me. Not the other way around. I knew I would have to shuffle things around to make it work, just like he did. I'm giving him the benefit of the doubt that he'd do what he needed to."

"I got it. Sorry."

"You don't need to be sorry. But I don't like seeing you hurting. And Tyler mentioned he's worried about you too. Are you okay?"

"I don't know." Emotions swirled around her, and she couldn't latch onto anything specific. Did Tyler really worry about her, or was he just saying that to Kyle? He had pushed her. But he had also been right. She needed to set some things straight with Kyle.

Kyle got up to leave. "If you need to talk, I'm here."

He was almost to the door, and she was going to lose her nerve. "Kyle, I don't want to do Happy Moments anymore."

"You don't have to do the speech. I can take care of it," he said.

"Okay. Thanks." She shook her head. "But that's not what I meant. I don't want to be in charge of it anymore. I love working on projects, and I'll still support you with it, but running Happy Moments isn't my dream. I want to go to New York. And work for *True Story*, or another big magazine."

Kyle let go of the doorknob. "How long have you felt like this?"

Liz bit her lip, and looked around. The words rushed out before she could recall them back. "Almost two years. I *wanted* to make it my dream. I really tried to. But it's not me. I love helping, and I love volunteering for the summer projects, but the management wears on me."

Kyle pulled Liz into a quick hug. "I wish you'd have told me sooner."

"You're not mad? Or disappointed?" She searched his eyes. "Are you disappointed?"

"I can't be mad that your dream is different from mine. I want you to be happy, Liz. If Happy Moments doesn't make you happy, that's okay."

"Really?" Her voice trembled.

"Really. I will find other people to help me. Why

didn't you tell me before? Had I known I never would have pushed you so hard."

"I didn't want to disappoint you. I didn't want you to think I wasn't supporting you and cheering for you."

He smiled. "You don't have to do everything I do, to show your support."

Tyler had been right. The thought made her head spin. "I know that now," she said.

"Go unpack. We have a long week of fun ahead of us."

Grip carried Liz and Cassie's bags to the third floor.

They unpacked their bags into dressers, talking through the bathroom that separated their Jack and Jill bedrooms.

A knock sounded at Cassie's door. Liz heard Grip's voice. "Hey, my mom asked me to run to the grocery store and pick up a few things for her famous cookie salad. Do you and Elizabeth want to come with me?"

"We're just settling in."

Liz strained to hear Grip's lowered voice. "We don't have a lot of time. We'll be in gridlock traffic soon. Maybe finish unpacking later?"

Liz stuck her head into Cassie's room. "Grip, we're almost done. Traffic should still be fine. Give us five minutes." She resumed putting her makeup into the bank of drawers on her side of the bathroom.

Twenty minutes later they split up to grab the ingredients at the store. Liz grabbed the lemon pudding, whipped topping and buttermilk and met Grip and Cassie to check out.

"Grip, it's only a double batch," she said as she surveyed the four packages of striped cookies next to the canned fruit on the conveyor belt.

"Who says they're all for the salad."

Cassie and Liz both laughed.

After ten minutes of only moving two blocks in traffic, Liz pulled out her phone. "I'm going to text mom and let her know that we're stuck in traffic. At this rate, it'll take us twice as long to get home."

"Check your messages too. Maybe you have a message from Tyler." Grip turned onto the freeway.

"Not likely." Liz glanced at Cassie. "I mean, maybe. But you know how we left it two weeks ago?" Liz's voice was tentative.

Cassie nodded. "I know enough, but not details. I'm sorry Tyler ran you off."

"He didn't run me off he, I, we just..." She let the sentence dangle.

Grip turned on the radio. It blared a Christmas song.

"I can't believe Christmas songs have been on since November first. Like we have to skip Thanksgiving as a holiday because as soon as trick or treating is over Christmas music plays." Grip didn't seem too put out by it.

"I like Christmas music." Cassie swatted Grip.

"I do too, it's just the timing is wrong," Grip grumbled.

The timing was all wrong. Just like her relationship with Tyler.

She clicked into her text messages. No new texts. She shouldn't expect it. Didn't expect it. But after talking with Kyle earlier, she hoped for it, though she didn't deserve it. Not after the childish way she stormed out and all the times since then that she refused to listen to his explanation. She knew her shortcomings. Not the least of which included pride and ego. And she was stubborn. And she had a temper. And she could keep going on, but why beat the horse to death?

Then she remembered the e-mail she received from Tyler, sent when she was talking with Kyle. It was still unread in her inbox. She clicked on it.

"Liz, Peter sent these to me. Here are your copies I promised I would deliver. Glad you arrived in Dallas safely. Tyler"

The sparse lines felt like a book that she couldn't put down. She wished that more would appear. How would he know if she was in Dallas safely? For a second she allowed her heart to thump harder at the thought that he was here.

But Cassie likely checked in with her family after landing. Perhaps Cassie mentioned Liz as part of the message, or Tyler inferred she was safe because Cassie was. Still it was a nice gesture, even if her heart pounded in her throat, that he cared for her.

She focused her attention on downloading the attachments, and clicked on them one by one, opening them on her small screen. She opened a half a dozen photos of her and Tyler together at the conference. The ones Peter took when he thought the play on words was funny—*Writers in Action*. Or something like that.

She'd smile if it didn't cause her heart to break a little more around the edges. A couple pictures of them kissing. A close-up. Another picture of them laughing together while studying her schedule. Another one of Liz sitting in the chair and Tyler coming toward her. She must be opening the pictures in reverse. She didn't remember this moment. Her head was bent over her schedule, and Tyler was in the distance. The smile on his face revealed the dimple on the lower left corner of his cheek. It was a smile that melted her, even on a two-dimensional picture. Finally, the last picture was one of them walking away from the camera, fingers entwined.

Emotions warred inside her. After talking with Kyle, she knew she had to apologize. Kyle was right. She couldn't hold Tyler's priorities against him. He had to do what was best for him, just like he advised her to do. But Alex calling the work they did on the charity together a mess, still stung.

She wouldn't apologize over the phone. It would have to wait until she could see him in person. It wouldn't guarantee a solution with Tyler. But hopefully he would accept her apology, and Christmas with her family wouldn't be weird with him there as the biographer.

Was it already too late to fix things? Liz tried to stifle her sob behind a sigh, but it didn't work.

"What's wrong, Liz?" Grip asked.

Liz collected herself. It wouldn't do to show up red-eyed and puffy faced. She shook her head. "Just got an e-mail. I'm fine."

Cassie turned her head. "You'll be okay, Liz. I know it."

"I miss Tyler."

"I have a feeling he misses you too."

She cringed. Cassie didn't know that he'd only been helping her to further his own plans.

"I'm not getting involved," Cassie continued. "Just a thought for you. Not something he's told me specifically."

Liz nodded. "Once more around the block while I add some concealer to my eyes."

"You got it." Grip took a left at the next intersection. "We'll take the scenic route back."

After an exhausting day of travel, compounded with dinner, games and general socializing, Liz wanted to curl into bed as soon as possible. The mounting tears behind her eyes threatened to spill every time she thought about Tyler. She splashed cold water on her face and massaged her eyes with a washcloth.

A soft knock came from Cassie's side of the bathroom door.

"Come in," Liz said.

"Do you mind if I'm in here at the same time as you?" Cassie held up a bag.

"Join me. How did today go for you?"

Cassie set her bag down on the counter and opened

another drawer containing her toothbrush. "I had a great time. Your family is so welcoming."

Except for me, Liz thought. *I'm the reason Tyler isn't here tonight.* She nodded in acknowledgment. "They *are* pretty great."

"They're *really* great."

"You like Grip, don't you?"

Cassie bounced on the balls of her feet, grinning.

"You're a good fit for each other," Liz said. "I've never seen my brother so happy or so excited."

Cassie's eyes widened. "Really?"

"Truly." Liz felt a pang of loss at not having the same. Her mind wandered again to Tyler for the hundredth time. Getting over him while Cassie was around would be impossible, but she smiled at Cassie anyway. It didn't lessen her pain, but she eased Cassie's anxiety about the weekend.

"Sorry Tyler isn't here. It's my fault, since I'm the one he's avoiding. If I could go back and change the last week, I would."

"How would you change it?" Cassie motioned for Liz to follow her into her room.

They sat down on Cassie's bed, and Liz let out a breath. "I wouldn't have jumped to conclusions."

"That's all?" Cassie's question didn't hold anything but curiosity.

Liz shook her head, unwilling to tell her specific details. "I wouldn't have pushed him away or let something else come between us." A corner of Liz's mouth lifted slightly as she shrugged. She had let Alex's words separate them.

"You like him a lot." Cassie squeezed a pillow and leaned closer.

"I love him a lot." *I thought I could have married him,* she added to herself.

"I knew it." Cassie squealed and pointed a finger at Liz. "You're so smitten. No wonder you've been miserable all day."

Her sweet voice brought the pricking of tears to Liz's eyes. She dabbed at them, and Cassie reached for the box of tissues on her side table.

"Thanks." Liz blotted her eyes and blew her nose.

They talked for another hour. Funny things about Tyler. Funny things about Grip. Moments that were worth melting over, and general girl talk.

Liz gave Cassie a hug. "Thanks for listening, Cass. You're a great friend."

"Cass is a pet name Tyler used to use." Her smile dropped as she looked at Liz.

"I'm okay now," Liz said. "It's been good to talk with you."

"You're like the sister I've never had," she said solemnly.

Liz nudged her. "Who knows, maybe I'll be your sister someday."

Cassie blushed. "Or maybe you'll be my aunt."

Liz's jaw dropped. "Well..." she stammered. *I wouldn't be opposed to that relationship either, but it won't happen now. Not after everything that's happened.*

234

Cassie squeezed her hand. "Don't worry about it. It's going to work out. You'll see."

She mustered a smile. No way was it going to work out. Not the way she hoped. "Good night, Cassie. Have a good sleep."

"You too."

"Liz?" Cassie called after her.

Liz stuck her head back through the bathroom door. "Yeah?"

"Would you mind if we talk like this again tomorrow night?"

Cassie's face was full of hope at such a simple request. "I'd like that. But come to my room."

Cassie grinned. "Okay. Hopefully we have more to talk about."

Liz stopped. Cassie would have oodles of stories to tell and questions to ask after going to Happy Moment's ball with the Montgomery family. "One of us will."

Cassie had a glint in her eye. "It's true."

CHAPTER TWENTY-FOUR

Tyler knew he was crazy. He stood in the dressing room, rotating his cufflink for the fifth time. His mind should be on his speech, but it kept wandering to Liz.

When Liz had told him that he was off the hook for the Happy Moment's speech, he felt like a rejected manuscript in the trash. He had nothing to say.

But then he had realized that Alex had planted the mistaken idea to Liz that Tyler was already booked for that weekend. But he hadn't been double booked originally, and he wasn't going to stand Liz up. Not after all the work she'd put in to redo this whole project. He wanted her to succeed, no matter what she thought of him. This was something she needed, and he wasn't going to let her down, even if she rejected his help.

He had rearranged his schedule, and even added extra book signings into the mix, to appease Alex. He'd been at signings at several bookstores in Dallas yesterday and this morning, but he was able to work in the speech tonight.

Earlier in the week Tyler had called Kyle to talk through the whole situation with him. He knew Kyle had an idea about him and Liz dating, but he explained it in detail anyway. He was still Kyle's biographer, and he needed to talk through the issue of not bailing on the charity ball.

Tyler had rambled to Kyle, still trying to make sense of why Liz was pushing him away. When he finished, Kyle had paused for a long moment. "Tyler. I want you to speak at the charity ball. If it works in your schedule, I think it'd be great for both of us if you presented."

"I told my agent I wasn't missing this commitment, no matter what the cost," he had said back. "But I don't know how Liz will take it. I don't want to hurt her. So, if it's better that I don't do the speech, for her—"

"I'll talk with Liz," Kyle had said. "And I'll see you on Saturday."

Tyler paced the small dressing room, waiting to speak at the Thanksgiving charity ball. Had Kyle talked to Liz? How had it gone?

He straightened his bowtie, and buttoned his jacket. His palms grew moist at the possibility that Liz might still announce him as they had previously arranged.

A knock sounded at his door. "I'm announcing you in five."

Tyler opened the door to see Kyle. "I'll be ready. Are you sure this is okay? I really don't want to step on Liz's toes. She sounded like she preferred to give the speech. I don't mind if she uses my notes."

"She doesn't want the speech. She actually doesn't want to work for Happy Moments anymore. It's a relief for her to not worry about it."

Tyler nodded. Good for Liz. "She told you?"

"Her unhappiness in Happy Moments doesn't come as a shock to you." Kyle lifted his eyebrows.

"It did the first time she told me."

"Well, at least we're all on the same page now. I'm going to miss her expertise, but she needs to focus her energy on her own priorities."

Tyler agreed. He was happy Liz was on the path to following her dreams, even if they didn't include him. He cleared his throat. "I'm going to go over my notes again. I'm sorry I can't stay for the entire night. Alex is waiting for me and we're catching a late flight after my speech. Next week is busy leading up to Thanksgiving."

Kyle shook his hand. "I know how that goes. Thanks for coming tonight."

"I didn't want to miss it."

Kyle nodded, and headed out the door.

Tyler fingered his note cards. He knew what he wanted to say. His mind caught hold of Kyle's revelation. Liz was done with running Happy Moments. That was a big step. He hoped what he'd said about Liz following her dreams the last day of the conference had a positive impact on her. He hoped she didn't do it because he thought she should.

Over the past two weeks he'd tried to connect with

Liz, but she hardly responded to text messages. Calling only resulted in leaving a message, and he'd stopped leaving them after a week. It was hard to reconcile, but she was following her own dreams.

He brushed imaginary dust from his sleeves. He wouldn't keep bothering Liz, hoping that she'd respond to him. It was time for him to move on too.

When they ran into each other at Kyle's functions between now and the Super Bowl, he would be professional.

But he needed to reframe the last few months. So, they'd worked on a project together for days at a time. He'd helped her out, but he'd really been helping Kyle out too. They'd kissed a few times. He thought that meant something, but... he lingered on the memories. Missing the feel of her in his arms. He couldn't reframe it. He had worked on the charity because of her. He missed her.

He shook his head, listening to Kyle's voice over the speaker in his dressing room. He pushed down the feelings he had for Liz as he opened the door into the backstage hallway. He'd be on soon. Kyle was thanking everyone for coming, running through statistics of the charity and talking about the silent auction that would be held following dinner.

Tyler half-expected to see Liz backstage. But she wasn't there. Kyle began announcing him, and he stood behind the curtain, waiting to make his entrance from the wing.

He came out and shook Kyle's hand, then took his

place at the mic. "It's an honor to be here tonight with all of you. Happy Moments is going to benefit from your generosity tonight. I'm here to introduce next summer's service project..."

He went through his prepared remarks almost automatically. He engaged with all sides of the audience as they ate their first course. He scanned the crowd. But still no sign of Liz.

He paused in his speech, clearing his throat. His plan to involve Liz would have worked better if she had introduced him. He finished up talking about the entire project, now he was going to give credit where it was due.

"I was introduced to Happy Moments this fall by Liz Montgomery. Liz? Are you around?" He paused, scanning the room back and forth. Movement came from one side of the room, and Liz glided through the side doors. His heart slammed upwards into his throat. "Liz, come up here for a moment."

Liz raised an eyebrow at him, but as the entire room turned toward her, she gave a slight nod, and made her way up the stairs. She was in an emerald green floor length gown that swished as she walked. He was glad the entire room watched her. It gave him an excuse to do the same.

She stood a few feet away from Tyler, her hand at her side, her fingers rubbing on her thumb. The only sign that she wasn't completely composed.

"Ladies and gentlemen, may I present the brains behind next year's summer project. This isn't public knowledge yet, but hopefully Kyle will forgive me for

240

giving you some insider information. Happy Moments' service projects are not put together overnight." The crowd laughed. "Not even close. They take two years of planning for each event. When the original plan for next summer fell through, Liz sacrificed her personal dreams and goals to put together this year's project I've just described, in record time. Without her tireless work and passion for what Happy Moments does, nothing would have been announced tonight. Let's recognize Liz for all of her time and dedication to Happy Moments." He stepped back from the mic, and started clapping loudly.

Cheers erupted from the room, and several tables stood, showing their appreciation. Liz looked at him, her eyes shining with gratitude.

When the clapping died down, Tyler said, "Liz, would you like to say a few words?" He held his breath, waiting for her to respond. He released it as she nodded. Tyler stepped back, but didn't move too far from the mic.

"Thank you," she said, her voice shaking with emotion. "The last few months of Happy Moments has created mostly stressful moments for me." The audience laughed. "But I'm thankful for Tyler Lakewood, who so graciously stepped in to help with the last-minute changes." She glanced back at him, and gave him a hesitant smile. "Happy Moments is dear to my heart. I love the traditions we have built each year as we've drawn together, united in helping others.

"Service has always been a big part of Kyle and Kandice's life. Though the service project is different this year, it will still carry with it the mission statement of

Happy Moments—*to create happy moments, one moment at a time.* Thank you for your continued support of Happy Moments as we strive to make each year better than the last. Create a happy moment tonight for someone else. Thank you, and enjoy your evening."

Liz stepped away from the mic as applause sounded through the room. Kyle came back out on the stage, shook Tyler's hand, and brought him into a hug, and hugged Liz. "Thank you both," he whispered. "This was better than I imagined it would be."

Tyler nodded to Kyle. Liz had brought down the house with her words. He was proud of her.

Kyle quickly announced the rest of the evening schedule, and then whisked Tyler and Liz off the stage.

Liz cleared her throat. "Thank you for your praise. It was...unexpected."

"I only said the truth." He kept himself composed. He gave the speech he'd wanted to give. And he hoped Liz would approve.

"I'm sorry for the way things turned out, but I'm glad you made it tonight."

"Me too, I—"

Alex ran down the hallway behind Liz. What was he doing? He was supposed to be waiting in the car. "Caught your speech, Ty. It was great. You were right. Lots of big donors here, and it's good that you didn't let them down." He put an arm around Tyler's shoulders, forcing him to walk with him. "Traffic is terrible. We need to leave if we're going to get out of here."

Tyler looked between Alex and Liz, blowing out a breath. "Just give me a few minutes. I'll be right there."

He turned back to Liz. Her eyes were hard. "Looks like we both got what we wanted." She watched Alex's retreating figure down the hallway. "Thanks for the speech."

"Liz, it's not like that. Let me explain—"

Helen came bustling toward them. "You two were all the rage!" She gave both of them a one-armed hug at the same time. "Liz, there are some people who want to meet you. I told them I'd bring you over straight away. Excuse us, Tyler."

"Let's talk later," Tyler called to her.

Liz glanced over her shoulder, but he couldn't tell if she agreed or not. She allowed her mom to lead her from the backstage area toward a group waiting for them. Tyler watched through the curtains, wondering who she mingled with.

He couldn't take his eyes off her, as she chatted with different groups. Someone tapped his shoulder, and he turned to see Alex again.

"You're going to miss your flight. Let's go."

He was close to blowing off the flight and firing Alex. But from the pained look on Liz's face, neither of those things would help him now.

CHAPTER TWENTY-FIVE

For the next hour, Liz was in a non-stop conversation. She felt like she was in a receiving line. Everyone wanted to come talk to her, asking her personal questions about what she gave up to make Happy Moments a success. Through it all Liz kept the approach positive, working a way to share that sacrifices were part of the way the Montgomery family did things.

Several donors wanted to share their personal stories with her too. Kyle came by a few times, and Liz directed some of the questions to him. She wondered if Tyler meant they should finish their conversation tonight? She had several things she wanted to say. Where was he? She needed to clear the air. At the core, she wanted to trust Tyler, to be with him. She needed to see if he meant what he said in his speech or if it was all for show. She wanted to believe him.

She excused herself from chatting, and walked

toward the center of the ballroom. This was now the second dancing function she'd been to with Tyler, and they still hadn't danced. She shouldn't care about that, especially after Alex's revelation.

A man in his early 30s came up to her. "Looking to dance?" he asked.

"I've seemed to have lost my speaking partner," Liz said, looking past the man. "Have you seen Mr. Lakewood?"

"Not recently."

"Are you enjoying yourself, Mr...?"

"I'm Brandon." He shook her hand. "I always enjoy charity events."

A donor. She should have accepted his offer to dance. She'd be careful not to brush him off too quickly, but she needed to find Tyler. Every moment that went by added more urgency.

He followed her toward the outskirts of the dance floor. "I'm interested to know about your sacrifice in getting next summer's project off the ground."

Of course he was. Just like everyone else. Had Tyler been less vague it would have saved her from having the same conversation over and over. But, he didn't have to mention it at all, and he put her in the best possible light for the last Thanksgiving ball she'd be in charge of. He'd given her a gift, really. And had made her look more noble and selfless than she felt. And thanks to his thoughtfulness, Happy Moments would likely get more donors this year.

But where to begin. At the same place as before?

She'd sacrificed school work, projects, time with friends, *True Story*, and for all intents and purposes, Tyler.

"The usual things. Time and social activities. A few assignments suffered." She thought of *True Story*. That assignment above all of them had suffered. "Tyler, er, Mr. Lakewood may have exaggerated his statements," she said finally.

He looked up toward the ceiling then met her gaze again. "I believe Mr. Lakewood mentioned something about your dreams and goals. What dreams were sacrificed?"

It was the first time all night a question had been so pointed, and it caught her off guard. She let her shoulders relax as she exhaled a deep breath. "You caught that part. You're very observant."

He gave a slight nod, but waited.

She shook her head. It didn't matter. Not really. Maybe it would help donations to the charity if she told the extent to which she'd sacrificed. Just because the internship at *True Story* wouldn't be hers, it didn't mean that she still couldn't get hired by them next fall. She still had a chance. At least that was what she told herself to keep composed. She only said, "There was an internship I'd worked for. But when crunch time came, I had to decide between it and Happy Moments."

"And you couldn't do both?" he pressed.

"The deadline for the internship conflicted with my narrow window to redo the plans on the project."

"So, you let your dream go then?"

In a manner of speaking, among other dreams. "I'd

246

committed to help my brother first. When push came to shove, I couldn't do both. The internship would have been great, but I couldn't give my application the attention it needed." *And when I realized my actual deadline was twelve hours earlier than I thought, I barely had twenty minutes to write my article.* But she wouldn't tell that to a stranger. Of course the writing she turned in suffered. It was her own fault.

"Are you happy you made that decision?"

The decision to focus on Happy Moments so much that at one point she was willing to drop her Masters classes to make it succeed? Liz smiled. "I can't change it. It was the right decision at the time." And now she knew that Kyle, or any of her family, wouldn't begrudge her own dreams. She just needed to be more vocal about them. Focusing on herself wouldn't diminish her ability to cheer for her family.

"Still, that *True Story* internship is a coveted position."

A few other guests came up to greet her. Her head swam. She hadn't said anything to the man about *True Story*, had she? She'd kept all of her statements purposefully vague all night. As she was pulled into another conversation, Brandon wandered away from the group that formed around her.

She still hadn't seen any sign of Tyler, and now she needed to track Brandon down. She didn't want it spreading that she'd been rejected from *True Story*. It wouldn't help her credibility in being hired by other magazines. Especially if any of them had people here covering the event. She'd delegated the entire guest list for tonight when she redid the summer planning.

Brandon. Brandon who? The name didn't ring a bell. Was he a friend of Tyler's who was fishing for information to see if Tyler had told the truth? Or a donor wanting to authenticate Tyler's story before he donated an extra amount of money?

She caught Brandon's arm as he moved across the dance floor. He turned toward her, eyebrows raised.

"Would you like to dance, after all?" He smiled at her, holding out his hands for her to accept.

She couldn't say no when they were in the middle of other couples dancing. She took his hands. "I didn't mention *True Story* to you, did I?"

"You didn't." He spun her on the dance floor.

"Are you a friend of Tyler's?"

"We know each other."

That explained it. "Oh." Tyler hadn't given the story out, but he had friends among the group. That probably made sense since some would come for his speech.

"Liz. I'm Brandon Nelson. I'm from *True Story*. You were supposed to meet with me and a few others at the Digital Quill Conference."

Liz closed her eyes tightly. "I caught an earlier flight home to..."

"Watch your brother play. I know. I received the message."

Hope bubbled up in her. Why was he here, seeking her out? He worked for *True Story*. Maybe *True Story* wasn't rejecting her after all. She'd get the internship.

The thought was squashed before it fully formed. "You're covering the charity ball for *True Story*."

"I am. *True Story* has taken notice of Happy Moments, and if the evening goes well, and next summer's service project turns out as amazing as it was presented, it will be featured as one of the Top Ten Charities in *True Story*."

Her heart soared for Happy Moments, even as it plummeted for herself. He was only talking to her to get the inside scoop, but Happy Moments deserved the attention.

"That's wonderful. You won't find many better than Happy Moments. I'd be happy to give you all of my research notes, and point you to my online articles. You can use anything that would be helpful to you. I've covered it extensively since Kyle founded it. The archives can still be accessed. Please let me know if you can't find what you're looking for."

"I think I've found what I need."

He wanted to do his own research. That was fine, too. She smiled as big as she could muster. "Good luck to you then." She turned to leave, as the dance finished.

"Hold on. I can't offer you the internship."

"I don't expect you to. I wrote my application in twenty minutes, with no polishing after I'd been up for half the night. And I blew you off in New York because I had a game to get back to."

His eyebrows lifted. "You really wrote your piece in twenty minutes?"

"That's all I could give it."

"You're even more talented then. Your writing portfolio you left at the Digital Quill Conference was impressive. As was your previous articles on Happy Moments that you submitted. It was your quick turn-around article that didn't shine."

"I'll keep that in mind for future submissions."

"We hope to hire you before you have time for future submissions." He smiled.

"I'm not sure I understand."

"Our internship spots for this summer are full. However, I am in need of two assistants to do special field work. I'd like you to head up writing on Happy Moments to start, and other charities as we add them to the list. As long as you can sound unbiased toward Happy Moments when you compare them to other charities."

Could this really be happening? Liz bit her lip. "Tyler put you up to this, didn't he?"

"He only said I should talk to you, and find out your story. We've been toying with the idea of delving into charity work from a ground level. I think this would be a good fit."

"I'm not comfortable using Tyler's connections that way. It seems unfair." But a glimmer of something burned inside of her. Was Tyler helping her because he still had feelings for her?

Brandon swept a hand in front of both of them, taking in the room. "Look around you." He lowered his voice. "This whole thing is networking. Networking and connections is the lifeblood of Kyle's charity. I talked to

Kyle. He didn't ask for a job for you, only expressed that you were interested in *True Story* still."

This is really happening. "I am interested. It sounds like a great opportunity."

He shook her hand. "I'm in town until Monday evening. If you have time, I'd love to sit down with you to go over the details."

"I'm sure I can arrange that. Kyle has an office we can meet in."

He pulled out a card from his suit. "This is my contact information. Let me know when you have a time."

Liz stayed on the perimeter of the dance floor, spinning Brandon's card in her hand. She might work for *True Story* after all. She could barely breathe without laughing. Where was Tyler? She wanted to tell him the good news first. And thank him.

More and more couples joined in dancing after bidding in the silent auction. Every time the band changed to a new song several people wandered to check their bids. It would be a successful night.

Cassie and Grip danced toward her. "You two look great," Liz said.

Cassie blushed. "Thanks. I talked to Tyler before he left. He was hoping to catch you, but you've been monopolized by so many people, he wasn't able to. He wanted you to know."

"He should have come over." She really wanted to talk to him in person.

"I don't think he wanted to interrupt. And he had a flight to catch."

"You did great up on stage today, Liz. You were a natural." Grip smiled at her.

"Thanks, Grip. Now go back to dancing, you two." She held in her excitement about the possibility of *True Story* until it became an official offer, but wished she could spill it all to Tyler right now.

After the ball, Liz was exhausted. She and Cassie had talked about the evening and the more they chatted at night, the more Liz liked Cassie.

Before turning off her light, she grabbed her cell phone. She needed to send a text to Tyler. *Thanks again for the kind words you gave me today. Brandon from True Story was there, and based on what you and Kyle had said, he offered me a job. I told him I didn't want a job if it was based on my connections, but he said that wasn't the reason. I'm really excited.*

She pressed send, then texted once more. *I hope you'll be around for Thanksgiving.* He was the biographer after all.

A short text came in a few minutes later. *Congrats on the job. You deserve it.*

He didn't respond about Thanksgiving. She sighed. She wouldn't beg him to come. But she felt like it.

The days between the charity ball and Thanksgiving went by in a blur. Liz met with Brandon and worked out the details of writing for *True Story*. It wouldn't be full-time until after she graduated, but it was a start—a foot in the door.

Liz helped Kandice get ready for a Thanksgiving feast with the others. With the charity ball over, a weight was lifted from her. She floated through the week, finding extra energy to help and have fun. She only wished Tyler would have taken her up on her offer to come for the Thanksgiving celebrations all week.

CHAPTER TWENTY-SIX

Thanksgiving Day dawned chillier than expected. The weather would warm up as the day progressed, but they brought their hoodies. Grip gave Cassie a sweatshirt, shirt and hat that matched the rest of the family.

Liz sat at the end of the row of their chairs. An empty seat next to hers that should have been Tyler's, mocked her. She rested a shoulder on the empty armrest, angling her body away from seeing the vacancy, hoping at any moment it'd be filled.

When her niece Linny was restless, Liz jumped at the chance to take the first quarter as "Lindsay duty," which equated to walking up and down the stairs with her, and running after her at top speed around concessions. This little girl did *not* want to sit still. And maybe Liz didn't want to either. Especially when she sat next to a seat she wished Tyler sat in.

During the second quarter Ron came to claim Lindsay, tempting her with a sippy cup and a blanket. "Thanks for your help with Lindsay," he said to Liz.

She waved his gratefulness away. "It was nothing. I love that little girl. Even if I'm no longer the favorite 'Awnt.'" Cassie and Grip had spent enough time with Linny over the past week at Kyle's house, that Linny started calling her 'awnt Cass.'

"Jealous? If only she'd become an aunt to her, eh?" He spoke in a conspiratorially low voice, though no one stood nearby.

She nodded. "Who knows, she may."

Ron raised his eyebrows. "Do you know something?"

She shook her head. "Nothing officially. Just that feeling in the air."

"Watch out then. If it's in the air, it could attack anyone."

She laughed. "Touché."

Lindsay started to whimper, and her dad rocked her back and forth. Lindsay's eyes fluttered, then closed. "Thanks for wearing her out. I'm going to enjoy the game if she stays asleep." He nodded his head toward the stairs. "Coming?"

"I think I'll get a few snacks before I head down."

Her brother raised his eyebrows. "You know you don't have to buy your own food here, right? We'll get a fill during half-time."

Liz rolled her eyes. "I remember how Thanksgiving Day works. Maybe I'll just get a soda."

She moved toward the concession stand. The second quarter barely started, but she was thirsty now. She could hold off on the snacks, but waiting until half-time when she could quench her thirst right now seemed too self-sacrificing.

"A small root beer please." She handed the cashier her card.

She sipped her drink as she headed toward the stairs. With a clear view of the field, she focused her attention on the game. She gripped the handrail tightly.

"Looks like this stadium stocks lids for their cups. Smart choice." A familiar voice came from the left side of her.

Liz's heart leaped and danced inside. She took a steadying breath as she turned slowly. Tyler, in a hoodie matching hers and the rest of her family, stood two paces away. He lowered his hood.

She swallowed hard, but her eyes stayed locked on his. "This stadium also has rules about standing in the aisle ways and blocking others' paths."

Tyler stepped closer.

Liz drew in a shallow breath.

"I didn't block the aisle." He took another step.

Liz arched an eyebrow, her insides going completely to mush. Good thing her hand was supporting her weight on the rail, because lid or not on the root beer, she knew she would be falling. Falling for him.

"My mistake," she said quickly, her pulse racing.

Liz caught the movement of Tyler's lips forming a small smile, revealing his delicious dimple. His mouth.

His lips. Their last kiss. All of it played before her. She pressed a fingernail into her palm, confirming with the sharp jab that she was awake. And here he was. In front of her. Outside of her daydreams.

"What are you doing here?" Her voice came out breathy.

"You invited me back to the Thanksgiving festivities. I assumed that meant the game."

"And the rest of the week you missed."

"I wasn't sure if it would be a good idea. We didn't finish our conversation on Saturday."

"Saying I'm sorry again is going to sound insincere. But I am. I shouldn't have jumped to conclusions."

Tyler nodded. "Alex is a self-serving agent. He's good at what he does, but sometimes the only way to get through to him is to remind him of the intrinsic value of a situation. But it came out wrong. And it's not how I feel. It's just how I manage him. I wasn't sure what to think when I got the cold shoulder. I knew I had to explain in person again. I'm sorry."

"Me too." She moved closer to him. "Where does that leave us?"

"Can we start over?"

Her stomach was in knots but she shook her head. "I don't want to start over at the beginning." She watched his face fall. "Maybe we can redo the last couple of days." She stepped closer. "But I don't want to start *completely* over." The crowd in the stands cheered at some play, but Liz hardly heard it above the pounding in her ears.

His face was some mere inches from hers, his eyes determined. "I love you, Liz Montgomery."

Her heart flipped at the words, and the realization that she felt the same way. "I love you, Tyler Lakewood."

In one swift movement, his hands were out of his pockets and around her waist. He pulled her closer and kissed her with all of the emotion that had kept them apart for the last few weeks, and all of the emotion that brought them back together. Liz wrapped her arms around his neck as she returned kiss for kiss, unaware how her small lidded root beer slipped from her hand and soaked their shoes.

She pulled away, but Tyler lifted her over the spilled drink to a drier section of concrete, kissing her again. She leaned into him, running her fingers along his smooth jawline. He held her closer, like he would never leave this moment.

"Better sticky shoes than cold feet," she said, when she was finally able to draw a breath. She was oblivious to everything around them. The crowded stadium, the fans probably watching them. All of it blurred into the background.

He laughed and his dimple appeared, urging her to kiss him again. "Too bad I didn't think to kiss you the first time you knocked me off my feet. It would have made the perfect story."

Liz smiled. "I don't need the perfect story. I want the right story."

"Exactly right." He bent down and kissed her,

pouring promises and dreams into the moment. Electricity reached her toes. And the cheering crowd in the background went wild.

THE END.

EPILOGUE

CHRISTMAS

The festivities of Christmas died down around the Montgomery house, and Liz and Tyler sat next to the large fireplace and Christmas tree, the only ones left talking. The lights from the tree danced around the vaulted ceiling, and Christmas music played softly.

"I have one more present for you," Tyler said, handing Liz a box.

Liz untied the red bow and slid open the gold box to find a dark leather book inside. The title, embossed in gold flourishing letters read: Our Book of Love—The Love Story of the Century.

Her eyes widened. "Your new book?"

Tyler grinned.

He hadn't mentioned anything about this one to her, though she knew that not every brainstorming idea came to her ears. Her fingers tingled with anticipation, as she opened the book to the title page.

In Tyler's neat hand she read, "To Liz. This is a book for two authors, not one. Write it with me? Yours always, Tyler."

She looked up where Tyler had been seated, but he knelt on one knee in front of her, a box in his hand. He opened the hinge to reveal sparkles and dreams wrapped up in one large solitaire diamond on a white gold band.

"Elizabeth Madison Montgomery, will you marry me?"

Liz's eyes widened. "Yes! Yes!"

He slipped the ring on her finger, and lifted her up, drawing her to him and kissing her until she melted.

"We may need a bigger book to write that story," Liz whispered in Tyler's ear.

"As many volumes as we need."

LEAVE A REVIEW

For any book to succeed, reviews are essential. If you enjoyed this book, please take a few minutes and leave a review on Amazon. It really helps other readers discover books they might enjoy. This is the best way you can say thank you to an author! Please leave a review of Mr. Write on Amazon. Thank you!

JOIN CHELSEA'S VIP READER'S CLUB

To find out more about future releases and receive a free book, you can Join Chelsea's VIP Reader's Club (http://smarturl.it/ChelseaVIPClub).

FACEBOOK as Author Chelsea Hale
    (http://smarturl.it/AuthorChelseaFBPage)

TWITTER as @chelseamhale
    (http://smarturl.it/AuthorChelseaTwitter)

WEBSITE (http://smarturl.it/AuthorChelseaWebsite)

SNEAK PEEK

And now, a special sneak peek. Chapter One of Camera Wars, Book Two in the Sundaes for Breakfast Romance Series.

CAMERA WARS

CHAPTER ONE

Coco Beaumont looked up from where she curled up on her favorite couch, laptop perched on top of the blankets surrounding her. The only light in the room glowed from the Christmas tree lights and her screen. Christmas music played softly as she worked on creating a wedding video of yesterday's filming.

"I'll be home for Christmas" played, and Coco paused. Her boyfriend Jeffrey had traveled over Christmas, and the thought that she still hadn't seen him since the semester ended stung. "You can count on me," the music continued and she stared at the two presents under the tree, waiting for Jeffrey to open them. She swallowed, realizing when she turned the song around, she hadn't gone home either for the holiday.

Christmas was a popular time to get married, between semesters and with the backdrop of the snow-covered Rockies in Colorado. Booking seven weddings as a wedding videographer in two and a half weeks didn't give her enough travel time to make it home to South Dakota this year, but she'd video chatted with her parents and brother on Christmas. It was almost the same.

She tuned out the song and its reference to mistletoe and kissing and everything she missed this year, and went back to editing. She needed to stay focused on completing these videos quickly so she didn't fall behind.

Yesterday's video footage was magical, with snow falling lightly around them as the bride and groom kissed. She couldn't have planned the moment better. The dusted snow on trees and their hair felt like stepping into a winter fairytale. She increased the contrast on the video, letting the snow stand out even more on the groom's dark tuxedo. He held his bride in his arms, spinning her around, letting the snow from her dress spray away from the beaded fabric. Coco sighed. It was beautiful.

Coco's roommate, Liz, burst through the front door. But the dim light couldn't disguise the change Coco immediately recognized in Liz. She saved the clip she worked on and pushed her laptop to the table.

Liz tried to act natural as she dropped her purse on the small table by the door, but Coco could see the energy wanting to explode from her. It was a subtle glow —the kind that graced all the weddings she filmed.

"You're getting married!" she squealed as soon as Liz turned around. "I know it, I just know it!"

"Way to ruin the surprise, Coco," Liz said, a slight

pout on her mouth. She tossed her red curls over her shoulder.

Coco smiled at the nickname on Liz's lips. She preferred being called Coco. It fit her much better than the formal French roots of Colette.

"Don't worry. I'm the only one here. I won't say a word ... but I want to see the ring." Coco held out her hand and pulled Liz closer to her. "Wow! If that isn't the biggest Alcatraz I have seen all year—and trust me, I check them all out."

"Alcatraz? A prison reference for wedded bliss?" Liz scrunched up her nose.

Coco giggled. "Not the prison part. It means 'a big rock,' and that, my dear," she said, holding up Liz's hand to let the light capture the sparkle, "is one big rock. Actually, *several* big rocks. Sheesh, girl. You're going to sink the next time you go swimming." She couldn't stop staring.

"Thanks for the tip. I'll take it off before I swim." Liz pulled her hand back. "Okay, okay. No need to drool over it. No giving it away when Mandy and Jenny get home. I want to be the one to tell them." Liz wagged a finger in Coco's face.

"My lips are sealed."

"Speaking of, you're home kind of early, aren't you? Weren't you out with Jeffrey?" Liz probed.

Coco shook her head. "His plans were delayed with the huge snowstorm. He thought it'd be best to avoid coming home to Denver, in case he couldn't make it out again in two days. And evening is the best time for me to be creative with my videos." She clicked her fingers across her laptop keyboard for emphasis. Her boyfriend traveled up to a month at a time arranging construction projects for Better Builders—a non-profit organization. She wanted to be a supportive girlfriend, but she wished he could have been around for the winter break.

Coco squinted as blinding light reflected off Liz's ring. Liz didn't seem to mind as she wiggled her finger back and forth.

"As I remember," Coco said, tapping the side of her dark chocolate pixie cut, "you said when there were wedding bells in your future, you'd let me do your wedding video."

"Yes. You are the most amazing woman with a camera I have ever known. I really, really want one of those sappy, magical videos. But I want it about me ... and Tyler ... and about us together in our journey of love." Liz laughed.

"They can be *kind of* sappy." *But when you're the one in love, it's not sappy, it's perfect.* Liz and Tyler were perfect for each other, but her thoughts wandered to Jeffrey. They'd been together years longer than Liz and Tyler had. A winter proposal was romantic—snow falling around them, sprinkling their coats like fairy dust.

She sighed, remembering her last conversation with Liz on the subject. "I wish you would let me gift the whole thing to you."

Liz waved her hand in the air. "The roommate discount is generous enough. Besides it's going to be a lot of filming."

Liz's wedding was three full days of events, parties, and meals in addition to the actual ceremony. Tyler was a New York Times bestselling author, and Liz's dad had been a legendary NFL superstar, so their wedding was bound to be elaborate.

Coco beamed. "I'm up to the challenge. Have you guys settled on a date yet?"

Liz shook her head. "Not yet, but it will probably be early summer. I did have a different idea about the wedding video I wanted to run by you. We were thinking of having a wedding video with us in different seasons and different backgrounds, you know, to capture some of the engagement. What do you think?"

"I haven't done something like that before, but we can experiment if that works for you. We can learn together and get an idea of what you both want."

Liz gave Coco a hug. "You have such an eye for style; I can't wait to see what you come up with. I think we will have our photographer come along, too. Are you okay with that?"

Coco smiled. "That's totally fine. It actually works out nicely to have photos taken at the same time. It keeps out the nerves of being filmed and makes for great video when you hold poses and then relax into action shots."

"We're thinking of trying for some shots with snow around. Maybe right after New Year's we can go up to Aspen for a few days? The hotel we're getting married at wants to give us a tour and talk through the wedding plans."

Coco nodded. Jeffrey was out of town until mid-

January. "I'll make it work. Let's just find a time when it's not too cold, but when the snow is perfect. There will be a few more of those days coming soon, I'm sure of it."

"I'm so excited for everything. I'm marrying my best friend, and I'm going to have the most amazing video, thanks to your generosity and talent. I can't wait."

Coco colored under Liz's praise. "Thanks. Your confidence means a lot. It's shaping up to be my favorite video so far."

Liz turned to her. "Why's that?"

"I love the people in the video, and they love each other, and I've seen your love come together. It's a magical thing." She said it with a winsome voice.

"Is that how you feel about Jeffrey?" Liz asked.

Coco's stomach flipped at just the mention of his name. She had dated him for two years in high school. He was a year older, and as soon as she had graduated moved to Colorado without a second thought so she could be close to him, and they'd started dating again.

"I hope so." She *wanted* it to be magical, but it was a little hard to tell when he'd been traveling so much since he'd graduated with his Bachelors almost two years ago. It seemed like he was gone more than he was there. But she loved him. He was her safety and security. "No one holds a candle to him." And that was the way she preferred it.

Coco closed her car trunk, shouldered her bag of camera gear, and carried her tripod. She walked quickly toward

Liz and Tyler, every step increasing her excitement. Breckenridge was one of her favorite places to shoot engagement videos.

"Hey guys!" She wrapped her scarf tighter around her neck. "I *love* this area. So happy you decided to stop here before we hit Aspen."

"This grove looks incredible," Liz said, bouncing on her toes.

Tyler glanced around. "The photographer should be here soon, but we can start without him."

Coco unzipped her bag and pulled out her camera. "Give me a few minutes to set up and we'll be ready."

She planted the reflectors in the snow, positioned Tyler and Liz in a casual cuddle on a rock, and then switched to a 50mm fixed lens.

"I'm ready," Coco announced. "Two things to remember: one, don't break the fourth wall. So, unless I tell you to, avoid looking directly into my camera lens. And two, music will be dubbed over everything, so feel free to talk and carry on a conversation. I'll be moving around you and giving directions. Any questions before we start?"

Liz laughed. "You sound like an official director, Coco."

"Director Coco. That *does* have a nice ring to it!"

She held the camera with the steady-cam rig, double checked her quality and ISO settings, and hit the record button. "For this first shot, I want you to relax. Look at each other and you can laugh or tell a joke."

A glow from the reflectors made the scene buttery

and soft. Focusing on both of them, she blurred the image on the manual lens, then slowly brought it back into focus just as Tyler smiled and Liz laughed at whatever he'd said into her ear.

Perfect.

She kept them in focus as she slowly moved to her left to capture the continuation of the shot. Both Tyler and Liz had participated in a video for Coco's Capturing Emotions class, so she knew they would be good on the camera, but they made being in love look easy. Just a few more steps until she was on the other side of the rock—a brilliant way to end the scene.

"Now look right here and smile." A bass voice said.

Her perfect moment disappeared when someone moved into her shot, where she had just been standing. Her entire beginning scene was ruined. She rolled her neck. *No big deal. It's never exactly right on the first try. We're bound to do this a few more times.* She hit the pause button.

"This is such a great backdrop. Let's get a few kissing shots. The lighting is great here." The deep voice said again.

She wasn't in the habit of noticing guys or how attractive they could be, but his tall frame towered over her five-foot-eight as she approached him. Dark black hair peeked out from his hat, but it was his light blue eyes that caught her off guard. They were almost iridescent. She shook her head at the thought of his bright baby blues. She wasn't attracted to them. She just wanted to see what they would look like through the lens of her camera. Maybe with a high-contrast filter.

"Hey. I'm Coco Beaumont." She stuck out her gloved hand.

He shook it. Her hands must be cold from the weather or his were extra warm from just arriving.

"Peter Jorgensen. Tyler and Liz's photographer. You must be Liz's roommate." His smile was warm, although the morning was still chilly.

"Here I'm the videographer. I need a few shots of them laughing before they kiss."

"I'm sure we'll have time for both. Did you see the way the sun is peeking through the branches? It's a great effect on a kiss." He took a few more shots.

Coco glowered at his back. Yeah. She saw it. She had set up the shot and added the extra reflectors to create the effect, thank you very much. But she needed the shot of them laughing first—the shot that Peter just ruined.

Coco's fingers slipped on the dials as she readjusted her settings. "Let's try that same shot again, and I'm going to go the other way." She expertly navigated the snowy ground as she brought the blurry scene into sharp focus on the love between Tyler and Liz. She walked around, got to the other side of the rock, and cringed as Peter stepped into her shot for the second time.

"Turn toward that small tree and smile." The rapid clicks on Peter's camera sounded like a woodpecker who was insistent on driving everyone insane.

Coco started back from where she was again. "Peter. I'm actually looking to get a specific shot, and you're in it.

Could you maybe just step over here so when I do my three-sixty around them I can get the whole shot?" She pointed to the opposite direction.

Peter looked confused. "I can't get a good shot on their photos from over there."

Coco took a calming breath. "I just need this shot and then we can move on and do the rest of the pictures and videos."

He shrugged. "Sure."

It only took three more times for Coco to get what she wanted in the opening shot. She walked slowly back toward her original position. She was fading back into blurring the video to match the beginning sequence when Peter stepped in front of her and bent low.

"Liz. That is the perfect expression. Don't change a thing; I'm just going to change me." Peter moved closer.

The incessant clicking of his camera sounded like nails on a chalkboard. She blew out a breath. He had ruined her shot *again*. She pressed the playback button to watch the clip in its entirety while Peter's camera click continued to irritate her.

The whole shot had been great up until the last ten seconds. She hoped she could salvage it. Right now, it was time to work on a different scene. She had a few other places in the Breckenridge Mountains to hit before going to Aspen for the rest of the week.

"You're starting to look a little stale on your faces," Peter said. "Try stretching your mouth a little, and don't hold your pose between pictures."

Coco reset her camera and carried her tripod and

reflectors to a spot not too far away. "For this next shot, I want you to walk toward me. Hold hands and don't break your hand hold until you're forced to as I go between both of you. Then, as soon as you pass me, join hands again, and I will still be filming."

She walked farther ahead of them and drew a line in the snow with the toe of her boot. "When you get to here, turn around and smile at me. We can try it a few times, and it will feel more natural every time."

Peter was on her right side, so Coco decided to turn left to continue filming the couple as they walked away from her. The plan would have worked perfectly, except Peter jumped into her line of sight, blocking her view of them turning around and smiling.

"This is a great shot," Peter said. "Okay. Now smile at each other and look like you're more in love. That's it. That's it. Now Tyler, go in for the kiss."

Coco rolled her eyes. She pressed the pause button. The poor button was going to get worn out in just the first hour of filming, and she had a whole week to look forward to. One more calming breath would keep her voice steady as she spoke. "We need to do this shot again."

Tyler and Liz made the trek through the snow back to their starting places.

"What was wrong with that shot? Those pictures were perfect," Peter said, looking down at the LCD screen on the back of his camera. "See?" He held the camera lens so she could see the photo.

"Glad your pictures turned out, but you stepped into

my shot. Again." She huffed. "You. Sit. There." She enunciated each word and pointed to a rock off the path from where she would film.

He blinked. "You wanted the entire walking scene?"

Could he get any denser? "That's what I'm going for. The entire thing."

"Okay. Walk with me then," he said.

"No. I'm staying in the same spot until they get to that line and turn around. You already got your perfect pictures. You don't need more from this angle." She pointed to the rock again.

Peter shrugged. "Okay. It seems like a strange shot to film, but I assume you know what you want."

"I do." She adjusted her settings, and they filmed it three more times. With any luck, she would have enough footage to make the perfect, magical shot.

Read CAMERA WARS now!

ACKNOWLEDGMENTS

Wow. So much work goes into writing a book, besides actually writing the book!

Ami was among the very first to listen to my crazy ideas as I proclaimed, "I'm writing a book!" Her advice and insight has been invaluable from the beginning. I have several friends who read early versions of this story and helped me make it better. Thanks to Alyssa, April, Dani, and Evelyn.

Special thanks to Jo, who not only provided encouragement but insightful feedback in an almost instantaneous way. Who critiques a full novel in less than a day, on a holiday weekend?! You're one of my favorites.

Thanks to my Beta Readers: Ami, Jen, Kim, Lorri, Natalee, and Shelly. You ladies are fantastic!

Thanks to my many supportive friends and family members who asked how writing was going, gave me a boost of confidence, and told me I was amazing. My mom, especially, has always been my cheerleader.

Thanks to my editors. Candice was brilliant in her ability to polish. Suzi made my story sparkle.

Thanks to the many amazing authors I have had the privilege to rub shoulders with over the last few years. I've been inspired by so many!

And, special thanks to David, who has helped me through so many parts of this story. Your support was so crucial during the crazy process of taking my story out of my head, and putting it on paper! I love you.

ABOUT THE AUTHOR

CHELSEA HALE can't remember a time when reading and writing weren't part of her life. She loves to travel to real and imaginary places, and take others along for the ride.

During the summer she grows a massive garden, and in the winter she enjoys an escape to some place warm.

Chelsea is passionate about writing (of course!), Broadway musicals, singing, and capturing life through a 50 mm lens. She bakes homemade whole wheat bread and blends delicious green smoothies.

She loves her chocolate and her ice cream topped with a mountain of caramel, watches romance movies until she has the words memorized, and loves watching people and characters fall in love.

In elementary school, Chelsea discovered her last name spelled backwards was D'LoveD'Not and said, "If I ever become a romance writer, I'm using this as my pen name!" (Who says that when they're ten?!). She didn't follow through with a pen name (yet!), but she's ecstatic to write and share the characters that have been in her head with others.

She is married to her Prince Charming, and enjoys

living her happily ever after on a daily basis. She and her husband have four children and live near the Rocky Mountains.

smarturl.it/AuthorChelseaWebsite
http://smarturl.it/ChelseaVIPClub

94446377R00160

Made in the USA
Lexington, KY
29 July 2018